For more **Humphrey** adventures, look for

Winter according to Humphrey

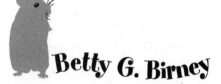

Betty G. Birney

G. P. Putnam's Sons
An Imprint of Penguin Group (USA) Inc.

G. P. PUTNAM'S SONS
A division of Penguin Young Readers Group.
Published by The Penguin Group.
Penguin Group (USA) Inc., 375 Hudson Street, New York, NY 10014, U.S.A.
Penguin Group (Canada), 90 Eglinton Avenue East, Suite 700, Toronto, Ontario M4P 2Y3,
Canada (a division of Pearson Penguin Canada Inc.).
Penguin Books Ltd, 80 Strand, London WC2R 0RL, England.
Penguin Ireland, 25 St. Stephen's Green, Dublin 2, Ireland (a division of Penguin Books Ltd).
Penguin Group (Australia), 250 Camberwell Road, Camberwell, Victoria 3124,
Australia (a division of Pearson Australia Group Pty Ltd).
Penguin Books India Pvt Ltd, 11 Community Centre, Panchsheel Park,
New Delhi—110 017, India.
Penguin Group (NZ), 67 Apollo Drive, Rosedale, Auckland 0632, New Zealand
(a division of Pearson New Zealand Ltd).
Penguin Books (South Africa) (Pty) Ltd, 24 Sturdee Avenue, Rosebank,
Johannesburg 2196, South Africa.
Penguin Books Ltd, Registered Offices: 80 Strand, London WC2R 0RL, England.

Published simultaneously in Canada.
Printed in the United States of America.
Design by Annie Ericsson. Text set in Stempel Schneidler.

Library of Congress Cataloging-in-Publication Data
Birney, Betty G.
Winter according to Humphrey / Betty G. Birney.
p. cm.—(Humphrey adventures ; 9)
Summary: Humphrey the hamster and the students in Mrs. Brisbane's
class get ready for the holidays and a special Winter Wonderland program.
[1. Schools—Fiction.   2. Hamsters—Fiction.   3. Winter—Fiction.
4. Holidays—Fiction.]   I. Title.
PZ7.B52285Wi 2012
[Fic]—dc23   2012005640

ISBN 978-0-399-25415-4
1   3   5   7   9   10   8   6   4   2

To my niece, Jennifer Powell Radman, and my nephew,
Todd Vincent Powell—

"Jenny" and "Todd" all grown up!

Contents

1

What a Lark

Humphrey! Where are you?" a voice called out.

I wasn't quite sure *where* I was, because I'd been sound asleep in my cage until I heard the voice.

My cage is a wonderful world all to itself. I have everything a hamster needs: a wheel to spin on, a sleeping hut, a climbing ladder, food, water, a mirror, tree branches and a corner just for my poo. (And that, of course, isn't near my food or water or sleeping hut.) And my bedding is like a lovely quilt that keeps me warm when it's cold in Room 26.

I poked my head out of the bedding.

"Oh, so that's where you're hiding." Mrs. Brisbane, my teacher, leaned down to look into my cage. I do like to play hide-and-squeak at times, but all I could think of that morning was keeping warm. During the winter at Longfellow School, they turn the heat down at night and turn it up again in the morning.

"Brrr, it's chilly," Mrs. Brisbane said. She was still wearing her heavy coat and a woolly cap. "I hope the heat goes on soon."

"YES-YES-YES!" I agreed.

But since I am a hamster and she is a human, all she heard was "SQUEAK-SQUEAK-SQUEAK."

"BOING-BOING!" my neighbor, Og, said. He's the other classroom pet in Room 26 and he makes a very strange twanging sound. He can't help it. He's a frog.

"Morning, Og," Mrs. Brisbane said, taking off her cap. "Winter is definitely here."

Soon my classmates began to arrive. They were all wearing heavy coats and hats, scarves and gloves.

"Hi, Humphrey-Mumphrey!" Slow-Down-Simon shouted as he raced into the room.

He'd been calling me that ever since we played a funny name game. I liked my nickname.

"Hi, Oggy-Moggy," Be-Careful-Kelsey called out as she passed by Og's tank.

"BOING!" Og replied.

Rosie rolled into the classroom in her wheelchair. She had a bright red cap and a bright red nose. "It's *cold* out there," she announced.

"It's *freezing* out there! It's twenty below zero!" Thomas T. True said as he entered. Just the thought of twenty below zero made me shiver and quiver.

I was about to dive under my bedding again when Mrs. Brisbane corrected him. "Thomas, it's actually thirty-five degrees *above* zero, which is cold, but not quite freezing. Now go hang up your jacket."

The students who had already hung up their coats stood around, talking.

"Wait until you see the present I'm making you," I heard Helpful-Holly tell Kelsey. "You'll love it."

"What is it?" Kelsey asked.

"It's a special surprise," Holly said.

Kelsey smiled. "Great!"

Holly turned to Tall-Paul, who was standing behind her. "I'm making you a special present, too," she told him.

Tall-Paul looked puzzled. "Why?" he asked.

"Because you're my friend," Holly said.

"You too," she told Small-Paul, who was standing next to Tall-Paul.

The two Pauls exchanged puzzled looks.

Then Holly came over to my cage. "Don't worry, Humphrey," she said. "I'll make a present for you, too."

"That's unsqueakably nice of you," I replied.

My squeaks made her giggle.

She turned to Og's tank. "I have a great idea for your present, Og."

"BOING-BOING!" Og twanged happily.

"I've got a big list of things to make," Holly said. "It's a lot of work. I even sneaked out of bed last night and worked at my desk with a flashlight. It's the only way I'll get them all done."

I wanted to get a present from Holly, but I didn't want her to go without sleep to make it!

The bell rang and Holly rushed to her table.

Hurry-Up-Harry arrived just as the bell stopped ringing, but at least he made it on time.

"Class, as you can tell by the weather, winter is here," Mrs. Brisbane announced after she took attendance. "And that means we've got to get busy practicing."

"We do?" I asked. I know I'm supposed to raise my paw before squeaking, but it slipped out.

"This year, Longfellow School is putting on a show to celebrate the winter holidays. It's called 'Winter Wonderland.' Each class will do a special performance that has to do with winter," she explained. "It takes place the evening before our winter break, and your friends and families are all invited."

Some of my friends went "Oooh."

Some of my friends went "Ahhh."

Thomas T. True said, "All right!"

I said, "SQUEAK," because when you celebrate something, it's usually fun.

"Ms. Lark will be in later this morning to tell you about your part in the program," Mrs. Brisbane said.

I'd heard of Ms. Lark, the music teacher. Sometimes the rest of the class goes to her room, but Og and I stay behind. My friends always come back humming.

Mrs. Brisbane changed the subject and passed out sheets of math problems.

I, on the other paw, kept thinking about the winter program. I know winter can be COLD-COLD-COLD. But it can be pretty when it snows.

But what on earth was a wonderland? I wondered what it would be like all through math class.

While Mrs. Brisbane was cleaning the board, the

door opened and in came a woman who almost looked like a student. She was slim with curly brown hair, and she was shorter than my tallest classmate, Paul Green. (I call him Tall-Paul.) She had a big smile on her face and she carried a stack of papers.

"Hello, Ms. Lark," Mrs. Brisbane greeted her. "We finished math class and are ready to hear about the show."

I scrambled up my tree branch and shouted, "Yes! Tell us now!"

Suddenly, Ms. Lark froze. "What was that noise?" she asked.

"Oh, that's our classroom hamster, Humphrey," Mrs. Brisbane said. "I think he wants to say hello to you. Would you like to come meet him?"

Some of my friends laughed, but Ms. Lark didn't.

She stared in the direction of my cage . . . and I think she shivered.

Mrs. Brisbane walked toward my cage, but Ms. Lark didn't follow. In fact, she took a step *back*.

Just then, Og said, "BOING!"

Ms. Lark backed up again. "What was *that*?"

"That's Og the Frog," Helpful-Holly said.

The music teacher's eyes grew wide and her voice sounded strange as she said, "You have a lot of animals in this class."

Mrs. Brisbane chuckled. "Yes, and they're not all in cages and tanks."

The rest of the class laughed, but Ms. Lark didn't even smile.

She kept staring in the direction of my cage until Mrs. Brisbane said, "We're all excited to hear about the winter program. Why don't you tell us about it?"

At last, Ms. Lark smiled and moved to the front of the classroom. "It's going to be an exciting celebration of everything the season has to offer. And I think Room Twenty-six has the best part of the show."

It's hard for a small, excitable creature like me not to squeak up when I hear something wonderful, but I managed to stay silent.

Og splashed around in his tank. I guess it was hard for him to stay silent, too.

"Your class is performing two songs. There'll be swirling snowflakes and prancing horses and jingle bells!" Ms. Lark's eyes sparkled.

"Oh, I love horses and bells!" I heard Sophie say. Then she turned to Kelsey, who was next to her, and started to tell her a story.

"Stop-Talking-Sophie," Mrs. Brisbane said.

Sophie said she was sorry and I think she meant it.

Rosie raised her hand. "Will there be real horses?" she asked.

"No," Ms. Lark said. "But there will be prancing and dancing and singing and ringing!"

All my classmates were excited at her answer.

"Yippee!" I squeaked. I didn't mean to, but it slipped out.

Suddenly, the sparkle went out of Ms. Lark's eyes.

"Does that hamster ever get out?" she asked.

"Sometimes," Mrs. Brisbane replied. "When he rolls around in his hamster ball."

This time Ms. Lark definitely shivered. And it wasn't even cold anymore.

"Could you explain how we're going to prepare for our musical numbers?" Mrs. Brisbane asked.

"We'll be rehearsing in here," Ms. Lark said. "The music room is being used to store the scenery for the show." Then she started talking about schedules and rehearsals and costumes.

My friends were especially excited about the costumes.

"Some of you will be floating snowflakes," Ms. Lark explained. "And some of you will be jingle bell horses."

There was a lot of murmuring in the classroom.

Og splashed a little louder.

"I'll be sending a letter home to your parents," Mrs. Brisbane said. "Now, let me say that this will be a lot of work and I want to make sure that you're all prepared to do your best."

"I WILL-WILL-WILL!" I squeaked, but luckily, I don't think Ms. Lark heard me because all of my friends were talking, too.

"Quiet, please," Ms. Lark said. Once everyone quieted down, she added, "It will be work, but it will also be fun and I know it will be *wonderful*! Now, I'm sure you all know the song 'Jingle Bells,' but there will be a brand-new snowflake song, too. I wrote it myself and I brought copies for you."

Helpful-Holly jumped up. "I'll pass them out."

Ms. Lark gave her the papers and Holly made sure all her friends had one.

All her friends except Og and me!

"I'll be working with you on the melody," Ms. Lark explained. "And one more thing: Does anyone in this class play the piano?"

Do-It-Now-Daniel's hand went up. "I do," he said. "I take lessons."

"Great," Ms. Lark said. "Would you like to play for the performance?"

"Sure," he said.

"I'll play the new song and I'd like to have you play 'Jingle Bells.' I'll get you the music so you can practice," she said.

Be-Careful-Kelsey's hand went up. "*I* take ballet lessons!"

I already knew that and I must say, Kelsey is a little more careful since she started ballet.

"That will be a big help," Ms. Lark said.

Thomas's hand went up next. "I play a musical instrument."

Mrs. Brisbane didn't look convinced. "Tell-the-Truth-Thomas," she said.

Thomas sometimes stretches the truth a little.

"I *do*," he insisted. Then he puckered his lips and began to whistle.

There are several things humans can do that I wish hamsters could do. Whistling is one of them.

Ms. Lark and Mrs. Brisbane both laughed.

"That's not a musical instrument," Mrs. Brisbane said.

"Sure it is," Thomas said. "My mouth!"

"I think we need that mouth for singing," Ms. Lark said.

Soon, the bell rang for recess and my friends ran to get their coats.

"Stay buttoned up," Mrs. Brisbane told them. "It's cold out there."

Mrs. Brisbane walked toward the door with Ms. Lark. "It will be hard work, but I know the children will love the program," Mrs. Brisbane said.

"I can see it now." Ms. Lark had her sparkle back. "A real winter wonderland."

After she left, Mrs. Brisbane came over to see Og and me. "You know, I don't think Ms. Lark likes animals very much," she said. "I feel sorry for her."

Poor Ms. Lark. I felt sorry for her, too. She doesn't know what she is missing.

HUMPHREY'S WINTER WONDERINGS: I wonder how an intelligent human being could *not* like a handsome hamster with long whiskers and beautiful golden fur.

Singing Snowflakes

After recess, my friends wanted to talk about the winter program.

Mrs. Brisbane, on the other paw, wanted to talk about science.

"I tell you what," she said. "Since you'll be singing about snowflakes, let's talk about them."

It turns out that snowflakes are SO-SO-SO interesting! I found out that:

- Snowflakes are made of little crystals of ice.
- Each snowflake has six sides.
- Snow forms in clouds where the temperature is below freezing.
- No two snowflakes are ever the same.
- Ice crystals form around tiny bits of dirt! Can you believe a beautiful snowflake starts with a piece of dirt?
- As they get heavier, the snowflakes fall toward the ground.

"If we're lucky, we'll get to do a science experiment with real snow," Mrs. Brisbane said. "What else can we do with snow?"

"Oooh, I love to go sledding," Sophie said. "We live on a hill and last year it snowed and all the kids in the neighborhood sledded all day. The hill was bumpy, so we bounced all the way down. And then my cousins came over and some friends and my mom made chili and we made popcorn, too. And then the next day . . ." Sophie paused for a breath.

"Thank you, Sophie," Mrs. Brisbane said quickly. "Who else has an idea?"

I don't think Stop-Talking-Sophie was finished talking. To squeak the truth, she never is.

She can talk more than any human I know!

"I like building snowmen," Holly said. Then she yawned a HUGE-HUGE-HUGE yawn.

My other friends came up with so many interesting things to do, like building snow forts and making ice cream out of snow.

I've never done any of those things because hamsters don't like the cold, despite our fur coats! Still, I enjoy watching the snow from the warmth of my cage indoors.

Then Mrs. Brisbane said, "And, of course, one of your songs is about the idea that no two snowflakes are exactly alike. I like the words to the song Ms. Lark gave us today. I think it's true for this class."

The words? *What* words? I wanted to get my paws on that song and find out what it said. After all, if I was going to be in the show with my friends, I needed to know my part!

Soon, all of my friends hurried off to lunch—except for one.

Holly was still at her desk, yawning.

Mrs. Brisbane noticed, too. "Holly, are you feeling all right?"

"I'm fine," Holly answered in a weak voice.

Mrs. Brisbane walked over to her table. "You seem tired today. Maybe you should go see the school nurse. Or I could call your mother to pick you up, if you're sick."

Holly yawned. "No, I'm fine," she said again.

Then Mrs. Brisbane did a strange thing. She put her hand on Holly's forehead. I tell you, humans never stop surprising me with their odd behavior!

"Did you bring your lunch?" Mrs. Brisbane asked.

Holly nodded.

"You can eat in here, if you'd like. It's nice and quiet. We could eat together," Mrs. Brisbane said.

Mrs. Brisbane brought her lunch bag over to Holly's table and they took out all kinds of yummy-looking food, like sandwiches and hamster-iffic carrot sticks. They didn't talk for a while as they ate. Then Mrs. Brisbane asked, "Are you all ready for the holidays?"

"Not really," Holly said. "I still have a lot of presents to make."

"It's nice to make presents," Mrs. Brisbane said. "But it's a lot of work."

"You can squeak that again," I said. "Holly's working so hard, she's not even sleeping. It might make her sick!"

I know that all Mrs. Brisbane could hear was SQUEAK-SQUEAK-SQUEAK, but I wished she could understand me.

"Who are you making presents for?" Mrs. Brisbane asked.

"Everyone in the class," Holly said. "Oh, and I forgot! I have to make something for Ms. Lark!"

Mrs. Brisbane looked puzzled. "We don't have a gift exchange in this class."

"I know," Holly said. "But I figured it out. I'm going to deliver them *outside* of class."

Mrs. Brisbane chewed a bite of her sandwich and then said, "That's nice of you, but why do you want to do this?"

"I love to make things! And I love to give gifts to show how much I like everybody," Holly said. "Then they'll like me back."

Then Mrs. Brisbane did something I don't see her do very often. She frowned.

"Holly, your classmates like you for who you are," she said. "You don't need to give people presents to make them like you. You know that, don't you?"

I was so glad to hear my teacher squeak up.

"That's right!" I agreed.

Holly thought for a moment. "I guess they do."

"It's important to get enough sleep, Holly," Mrs.

Brisbane said. "You don't want to get sick for the holidays."

It's amazing! Even if she didn't understand what I said, Mrs. Brisbane seemed to know what I was thinking. I guess that's what makes her such a great teacher.

Holly yawned again.

Mrs. Brisbane and Holly chatted a little more while they finished lunch. Then my teacher said, "Why don't you put your head on your table and rest until the others come back?"

"Couldn't I work on making my presents instead?" Holly asked. "I brought some of my projects with me."

Mrs. Brisbane shook her head. "No, Holly. Please drop the idea of making presents for everyone. Put your head down and rest."

Holly agreed, and soon she was fast asleep.

∾ ⸰∾⸰

Of course, Holly woke up when our friends came back into the class. (Maybe she didn't wake up all the way, though.)

Later in the day, Mrs. Brisbane read to us from a wonderful book about a girl named Alice falling down a rabbit hole (which sounds terrifying to a small creature like me). And just like our program, it took place in a *wonderland,* but not the kind where it snows.

It was hard to follow the story, though, because while Mrs. Brisbane was reading, Holly kept yawning and they kept getting longer and longer.

Yawn. Yawn. Yawwwwn. Yawwwwwwwn.

Then I noticed something funny. Once Holly started yawning, all the other humans in the room began to yawn.

Even *I* started to yawn, and I'm not a human.

I finally crawled into my sleeping hut for a nap. I was only sorry that Holly couldn't fit in there, too!

~·∾·~

"Og, do you remember the time you and I got snowed in?" I asked my neighbor that night when the school was empty.

"BOING-BOING!" Og replied.

"It doesn't seem that long ago," I said. "In fact, it was earlier this year. But so much has happened since then. And now winter is back!"

"BOING?" Og sounded surprised.

"I wonder if it will snow again. I wonder what a wonderland looks like. And I wonder what that snowflake song is like," I squeaked.

Og splashed around in his water a little, but he didn't answer my questions.

It was beginning to get dark in Room 26, but my hamster eyes see well in the dark. And as I looked across the room, I noticed a sheet of white paper under Be-Careful-Kelsey's table.

"I wonder . . . ," I squeaked. "Og, do you think that's a copy of the snowflake song?"

Og splashed a little louder.

I was thinking about opening the lock-that-doesn't-lock on my cage and trying to read the paper when I heard a familiar RATTLE-RATTLE-RATTLE coming down the hall outside the classroom.

The first time I'd heard that rattling, I'd thought a ghost was coming. But now I knew that it was only Aldo coming in to clean. He isn't anything like a ghost, thank goodness.

Suddenly, the door swung open and bright light filled the room as Aldo appeared, pushing his cleaning cart.

"Never fear . . . 'cause Aldo's here," his voice boomed out.

"Greetings, Aldo!" I squeaked at the top of my tiny lungs.

"Hello, Humphrey! Hello, Og! How are my favorite classroom pets?" he said.

I was glad we were his favorites. George, the frog with the deep voice in Miss Loomis's class, isn't one bit friendly. Sometimes it's difficult to understand Og, but I don't understand the hermit crabs in Miss Becker's room at *all*.

I've liked Aldo since my first night in Room 26. It was fun to watch him, especially when he showed me his trick of balancing a broom on his fingertip.

Aldo came over to our table and bent down so his face was level with my cage and Og's tank. I love to see Aldo up close because he has a big furry black mustache that wiggles when he talks. Sometimes I wonder if he stores extra food in there, the way I do in my cheek pouch.

"Say, have you heard about this Winter Wonderland show?" he asked. "It's going to snow in the gym . . . and that's no joke! Get it? *That snow joke.*"

When he laughed, his mustache shook.

It made me cold to think of snow outside. But the thought of snow *inside* the school made my teeth chatter.

"Here's a snow joke for you," Aldo said. "How do snowmen travel around?"

I had no idea, so I was happy when Aldo said, "By icicle! Get it? An icicle, like a bicycle."

"That's funny," I squeaked.

"Here's another one," Aldo continued. "What do you call a snowman in the summer? A puddle!"

Aldo's mustache shook even harder as he laughed at this joke—along with me.

Then Aldo went to work cleaning the classroom. He dusted the tables and was careful not to disturb anything on Mrs. Brisbane's desk. Aldo admires Mrs. Brisbane (so do I). He's even going to school to learn to be a teacher like her someday.

Next, Aldo got out his broom and started sweeping.

I climbed up to the top of my tree branch so I could have a better look.

He had collected quite a pile of dust and paper trimmings by the time he reached the piece of paper near Kelsey's table.

He bent down and picked it up. "What's this?" He studied the paper. "Oh, it's a song. Hey, I'll bet this is the song for the winter show."

"What's it say?" I squeaked loudly.

"BOING-BOING-BOING!" Og twanged excitedly.

Aldo started to whistle. I'm not quite sure how he did that, because I couldn't see his mouth under that big floppy mustache.

"I like it," he said. "That's a nice idea."

"PLEASE-PLEASE-PLEASE bring it over here!" I squeaked.

I guess Aldo didn't understand, because he put the paper back on Kelsey's table.

After he finished his work and the tables were in neat rows again, he pulled a chair up next to my cage and took out his dinner. He always eats his dinner with Og and me.

"Richie said his class is going to build a snowman in the gym," Aldo told us.

Richie is Aldo's nephew. He was in Room 26 with me last year.

Aldo chuckled. "Now that's something, isn't it?"

"It certainly is!" I squeaked. It would have to be COLD-COLD-COLD in that gym if they didn't want the snowman to melt. I shivered a little.

"I like that snowflake song, though." Aldo pushed a crunchy piece of lettuce between the bars of my cage.

"Sing it to us, Aldo," I said.

He didn't sing but he hummed a little. Then he sang, "Each one is special, just like me and you."

Aldo chuckled again. "I guess you two snowflakes aren't alike at all," he said. "And you're both special, all right."

After he finished his meal, Aldo threw a few Froggy

Food Sticks into Og's tank. My friend took a deep dive in the water to catch them.

Before I knew it, Aldo had rolled his cart out into the hallway and turned off the lights.

"Night, night," he said before closing the door.

The room was dark and quiet. I waited until I saw Aldo's car leave the parking lot a little later. Then I jiggled the lock-that-doesn't-lock on my cage and scrambled over to Og's tank.

"Did you hear that, Og?" I asked. "He called us snowflakes!"

"BOING-BOING!" he said.

"And he said we're special. I guess that's what the song says," I explained.

I glanced at Kelsey's table and saw the paper lying there. "I wish I could go over there and read it," I said.

Since I've been the classroom pet in Room 26, I've learned to read. I can even write in the little notebook hidden behind my mirror.

And I've learned to open my lock-that-doesn't-lock, get out of my cage and explore Room 26 at night.

But there was no way that I could get from my cage to Kelsey's tabletop, because I can't shimmy up such a tall, smooth leg. And I couldn't leap from her chair to the table because her chair was pushed all the way in.

"I guess we'll have to wait until tomorrow," I squeaked to my neighbor. It was suddenly getting chilly in Room 26. I looked forward to burrowing down in my nice warm bedding.

"BOING-BOING," Og answered.

It sounded as if he agreed with me, so I said good night and went back to the comfort of my cage.

Hamsters are often wide awake at night, so I had plenty of time to think.

If the students in Room 26 were snowflakes, certainly no two were alike. Slow-Down-Simon was always in a rush, while Hurry-Up-Harry was often late. Do-It-Now-Daniel put things off, while Helpful-Holly did everything right away. One Paul was tall and the other Paul was short. Oh, and Stop-Talking-Sophie was the complete opposite of quiet Speak-Up-Sayeh from last year's class.

Even the classroom pets, Og and I, were as different as night and day.

I have beautiful golden fur. He is green and has no fur at all.

He likes water and I should NEVER-NEVER-NEVER get wet.

I say "SQUEAK" and he says "BOING!"

And those are only a few of our differences.

I guess I wasn't wide awake after all because I drifted off to sleep and dreamed about snowflakes and jingle bells and prancing horses.

HUMPHREY'S WINTER WONDERINGS: Could there possibly be any two snowflakes as different as Og and me?

Jingle Jangle

I had to wait two days before Ms. Lark came back again. Then, before she arrived, the morning seemed unsqueakably long.

First, we had to do math problems. One was about a train going east and a train going west and as far as I could figure out, those two trains were going in circles!

Then, there was the vocabulary test. I hid in my sleeping hut with my notebook and took the test with the rest of the class. I'm sorry to say I missed three words. First was "drizzle." I thought it only had one *z*. I should have known it had two. After all, Mrs. Brisbane once gave us a made-up word, "furzizzle," and *that* had two *z*s.

Next was "frozen." I thought it had two *z*s. I also missed "icicle." I got carried away and wrote "icicicle." (I guess Mrs. Brisbane was using our spelling to get us in the mood for the Winter Wonderland show.)

"Og, do you think Ms. Lark is really coming back today?" I squeaked to my neighbor when we were alone in the room during recess.

Og splashed a little but he didn't answer. I guess he didn't know, either.

But once my classmates were back and in their chairs, the door swung open and Ms. Lark came in. She gave a nervous glance in the direction of my cage, then moved to the front of the classroom. She was carrying a piano keyboard with her. It was just the keyboard part—not the whole piano.

"Did you have a chance to look at the snowflake song last night?" she asked, placing the keyboard on the desk.

My friends all nodded, even Forgetful-Phoebe, who sometimes doesn't remember her homework.

"Great," Ms. Lark continued. "Let's warm up by singing a chorus of 'Jingle Bells.' Then I'll teach you the new song."

She flipped a switch and started playing the keyboard. It may have been small, but it was LOUD-LOUD-LOUD.

My classmates began to sing and I squeaked along.

Jingle bells, jingle bells, jingle all the way,
Oh, what fun it is to ride in a one-horse open sleigh—ay!
Jingle bells, jingle bells, jingle all the way,
Oh, what fun it is to ride in a one-horse open sleigh!

It's a happy song and I loved it so much, I kept on going.

Squeak-squeak squeak, squeak-squeak squeak.
Squeak . . .

Just then, I noticed that the rest of the class had stopped singing. My friends sitting near my cage giggled.

I stopped singing.

Ms. Lark looked in my direction and frowned.

But then she forced a smile (it looked forced to me) and told my friends what a good job they'd done.

Next, we sang the verse of the song. I didn't know that part, so I listened.

Dashing through the snow, in a one-horse open sleigh,
O'er the fields we go, laughing all the way.
Bells on bobtail ring, making spirits bright,
What fun it is to ride and sing a sleighing song tonight!
Oh . . .

When they went back to singing the "jingle bells" part, I joined in again. But this time, I remembered to stop when my friends did.

Ms. Lark explained what some of the words meant, which was quite surprising.

I'd thought that the horse's name was Bob and that he had bells on his tail. That's why the song said "Bells on Bob's tail ring." But I was WRONG-WRONG-WRONG! The horse's tail was cut short so it wouldn't

23

get caught in the reins, and that was called a bobtail. OUCH!

(I have a small tail myself, but I'm not sure how I feel about putting bells on it.)

"I want you to practice the song on your piano when you get home so we can rehearse with you playing soon," she told Daniel.

"Okay," he said.

"You will remember, won't you?" Mrs. Brisbane asked. "Tonight."

Mrs. Brisbane often had to remind Daniel not to put things off.

Then Ms. Lark moved on to the new song about the snowflakes.

I could tell my friends were as excited as I was to hear a brand-new song. They leaned forward in their chairs to listen.

I scrambled up to the tippy-top of my cage so I could watch Ms. Lark sing and play. She had a lovely voice. And I liked the words of the song, too.

No two snowflakes are the same,
Though they're lacy white.
No two snowflakes are alike,
Almost . . . but not quite.

Each one is special,
That is true.

Each one is special,
Just like me and you.

Snowflakes floating through the air
Make a lovely sight.
No two snowflakes are alike,
Almost . . . but not quite.

Each one is special,
That is true.
Each one is special,
Just like me and you.

Snowflakes covering the ground
Make the whole world bright.
No two snowflakes are alike,
Almost . . . but not quite.

Each one is special,
That is true.
Each one is special,
Just like me and you.

By the time she got to the end, the whole class joined in on the chorus. I wanted to, but I managed *not* to squeak because I was afraid I'd upset Ms. Lark.

When she stopped, Mrs. Brisbane applauded and everyone joined in.

"That's a beautiful song," our teacher said.

"Thank you," Ms. Lark replied. "But now I'll tell you the best part. Half of the class will be prancing horses for 'Jingle Bells.' Those students will wear tails, horse manes and bells."

"I want to be a jingle horse!" Stop-Talking-Sophie blurted out.

By the nods and whispering, I could see that the rest of the class wanted the same thing.

"The other half of the class will be glittering snowflakes whirling around the stage for the second song," Ms. Lark said.

"Oh, I want to be a snowflake!" Sophie exclaimed.

"Sorry, but you can't be a horse *and* a snowflake," Ms. Lark told her.

Sophie looked disappointed, but she was quiet for once.

"I don't want to be a snowflake," Simon said. "I'd rather be a horse."

All the boys nodded and said they wanted to be horses.

Ms. Lark turned to Mrs. Brisbane. "What do you think?"

Mrs. Brisbane thought for a second and then said she thought it would be a good idea if the girls were snowflakes and the boys were horses.

"Did you hear that, Og?" I said. "Since we're boys, I guess we get to be horses."

Being a horse wouldn't be that hard for a hamster. After all, unlike humans, I already have a tail.

"BOING!" Og twanged loudly.

The class practiced the new song several times and then it was lunchtime.

When the classroom was empty again, I burrowed under my bedding to warm up and to think.

I was thinking that Og wouldn't make a very good horse.

I'd never seen a picture of a green horse before.

And horses don't hop.

Still, I was HAPPY-HAPPY-HAPPY that we boys were going to be horses and I'm sure Og was, too.

※ ❦ ※

For the rest of the day, it was hard to concentrate on our studies, because I kept hearing "Jingle Bells" and the snowflake song going round and round in my brain.

Late in the afternoon, Mrs. Brisbane began talking about real snowflakes again. *That* got my attention.

Our teacher had started to explain how the ice crystals formed when Small-Paul Fletcher raised his hand.

"Mrs. Brisbane," he said when she called on him, "I did some reading about snowflakes last night and I found out that something we talked about on Tuesday is wrong. And Ms. Lark's song is wrong."

"Wrong?" Mrs. Brisbane looked puzzled.

Paul pushed up his glasses. "Yes, ma'am. The song says no two snowflakes are alike, but that's not true."

Not true? What was Paul saying?

"Oh, my! Has anyone seen two that are alike?" Mrs. Brisbane asked.

"I'm not sure about that," Paul said. "But it's scientifically *possible* that there could be two identical snowflakes."

"I see," Mrs. Brisbane said. "If you'd like to do a little more research on that, I'd appreciate it, Paul. Can you report back to the class tomorrow?"

As soon as Paul said he would, more hands were raised.

"Maybe we should change the song," Helpful-Holly suggested.

Mrs. Brisbane smiled. "I'm not sure that singing 'Sometimes two snowflakes might be alike' would sound as good, are you?"

"You'd have to change all the words," Thomas said.

"Does this mean we can't have glittery snowflake costumes?" Rosie asked. She looked VERY-VERY-VERY disappointed.

"You can still have glittery snowflake costumes," Mrs. Brisbane said. "And I think we can keep the song as it is. We'll talk to Ms. Lark about it tomorrow."

All of my friends seemed pleased with her answer.

"Speaking of tomorrow, whose turn is it to take Humphrey home for the weekend?" Mrs. Brisbane asked.

I looked around the room. Which house would I be visiting for the weekend? Each week it's a different place, which makes my life interesting.

Holly waved her hand wildly. "It's me!" she said.

"Don't forget to bring in the permission slip tomorrow," Mrs. Brisbane told her.

I was pretty sure that Helpful-Holly wouldn't forget!

Later that night, when Og and I were alone, I opened the lock-that-doesn't-lock and scampered over to his tank.

"Og, since we're boys and we'll be jingle horses, do you think we should practice singing 'Jingle Bells'?" I asked.

My friend didn't answer, so I decided to practice by myself. "Jingle bells, jingle bells, jingle all the way . . ." I began.

I was happy when Og chimed in. "BOING-BOING BOING, BOING-BOING BOING, BOING-BOING BOING BOING BOING!"

It didn't sound like "Jingle Bells," but at least Og was trying his best.

Later, I snuggled under the bedding in my cage with the notebook and pencil I keep hidden. I tried to draw two snowflakes that were exactly alike, but you know what? I couldn't do it!

I liked the idea that no two snowflakes—and no two people or hamsters or frogs—are exactly alike. I knew that Small-Paul was smart and knew a lot about science, but was he right about this?

HUMPHREY'S WINTER WONDERINGS: Are any two hamsters ever alike? It's STRANGE-STRANGE-STRANGE to think that somewhere there might be a classroom hamster named Humphrey who's just like me!

Sour Notes

I was on pins and needles until Friday, waiting for Ms. Lark to come back.

Would she be upset when she found out that the words to her song were wrong?

Would the girls be upset if she said they couldn't be snowflakes after all?

Would everyone be upset with Small-Paul for ruining the whole song? Would I?

"Ms. Lark, Paul Fletcher did some research and found that there's a problem with one of the lines in your song," Mrs. Brisbane explained when the music teacher arrived. "It *is* possible for two snowflakes to be identical."

Ms. Lark looked surprised. "Really? That's not what I learned in school."

Mrs. Brisbane called on Small-Paul to explain.

"What I read said that while there probably have never been two snowflakes that are alike, there is a *possibility,*" he said. "And of course, who would know for sure? Because you'd have to look at every snowflake that ever fell."

"Wow, that's a whole lot of snowflakes," Thomas said.

Ms. Lark blinked a few times as she thought. "Let's take a vote," she said at last. "Raise your hand if you think we should change the song."

Not one hand—or paw—went up. Even Small-Paul didn't raise his hand.

"Good," Mrs. Brisbane said. "And I think I have an idea that will make everything clear. I'll tell you later. For now, I'll let you sing."

And SING-SING-SING we did as Ms. Lark played on her keyboard.

First the boys sang all of "Jingle Bells." I squeaked right along with them, but I think they drowned me out.

Then the girls sang "No Two Snowflakes Are Alike." I didn't squeak along with them, since I'm not a girl. Instead, I hopped on my wheel and spun to the music.

I forgot one thing, though. My wheel makes a noise. It's not a little SQUEAK-SQUEAK-SQUEAK like mine, but a loud SCREECH-SCREECH-SCREECH. The more I spin, the more it screeches.

Suddenly, Ms. Lark looked up and stopped playing the music.

Some of the girls kept on singing, until they noticed she had stopped.

Ms. Lark stared in the direction of my cage, so I stopped spinning my wheel as well.

"Is that the—?" she asked.

"Oh, that's Humphrey's wheel. He enjoys spinning to music," Mrs. Brisbane said.

"So do I," Rosie said as she spun her wheelchair in a circle.

"Can we cover the cage with a cloth or something?" Ms. Lark asked. "So we don't have to hear him?"

Cover my cage with a cloth? Could my tiny hamster ears actually have heard those words?

"Oh, no!" Sophie gasped. "He'd feel terrible if you did that!"

I was so happy that someone knew I wouldn't like that!

"I don't think we need to cover his cage," Mrs. Brisbane said. "Let's just sing a little louder."

I was so worried that Ms. Lark would cover my cage, I didn't squeak—or screech—at all as the boys practiced "Jingle Bells" again.

They sounded fine to my small ears.

But Ms. Lark stopped again and said, "Who's that?"

The singing ended again.

"It wasn't me," I squeaked.

After all, I can't be blamed for everything!

"Sing again, boys," she said. "This time I won't play."

The boys cheerfully repeated "Jingle Bells." But this time, Ms. Lark walked away from the keyboard and stood in front of the boys, looking hard at each one.

When she was standing in front of Just-Joey, she frowned.

"I'm afraid it's you, Joey," she said.

The boys stopped singing.

"What did I do?" Joey asked.

"I'm afraid your singing is a little bit off-key. In fact, I'm afraid your singing was way off-key," she said.

"Off-key?" he said.

"Yes," Ms. Lark said. "You're not singing the right notes. Could you sing more softly?"

Joey nodded.

When the boys started singing again, Joey didn't just sing more softly. He didn't sing at all. His mouth was closed and he stared down at his feet.

It was the saddest "Jingle Bells" I ever heard.

∿•∿

"Poor Joey. I think he felt terrible about singing off-key," Mrs. Brisbane told Ms. Lark when my friends left for recess.

"I hated to say anything," Ms. Lark answered. "But Joey's singing was awful. He almost sounds like that frog over there. He's so off-key, he'll throw everyone else off, too."

"I'm sure he'll try to do better," Mrs. Brisbane said.

"He certainly will!" I squeaked.

Ms. Lark sighed. "I know, but will he be better by the time of the show? It's very important to me."

"BOING-BOING-BOING!" Og twanged.

I don't blame him for sticking up for frogs (although I have to admit, the sounds Og makes don't sound much like singing).

Ms. Lark shuddered as she glanced over at Og and

33

me. "Don't those animals bother you while you're teaching?" she asked.

"Not a bit," Mrs. Brisbane said. "The children learn a lot from them."

"And *you* could learn a lot from Mrs. Brisbane," I squeaked. If only humans could understand me—at least once in a while!

I'm not quite sure Ms. Lark believed Mrs. Brisbane . . . or me.

"They won't . . . bite?" she asked in a shaky voice.

"Og certainly doesn't. And Humphrey doesn't, either, though some hamsters may give you a nibble if they're scared. It's not *their* fault," she said.

I'm not sure, but I think Ms. Lark squeaked. She might not like hamsters, but she sounded like one!

"They won't hurt you," Mrs. Brisbane said. "Now, why are you so worried about the show?"

"It took a lot of hard work to convince Mr. Morales to let us have a winter program," Ms. Lark said. "Finally, he said we could try it this once and see how successful it is. So I want everything to be perfect."

Mr. Morales is the principal and the Most Important Person at Longfellow School. So naturally, Ms. Lark would want him to be pleased.

Mrs. Brisbane put her arm around Ms. Lark's shoulders. "I do understand, Mary. But try to relax. I know the children won't let you down. And the parents will love the show."

"They will!" I squeaked.

"BOING-BOING!" Og agreed.

Ms. Lark left, thank goodness. But for the rest of the day, I thought about Joey. I didn't think he, or his family, would enjoy the show if he didn't get to sing.

And once we were alone at the end of the day, I opened the lock-that-doesn't-lock on my cage and hurried over to Og's tank.

"I'm sorry about what Ms. Lark said about your croaking," I said. "I thought you and Joey sounded GREAT-GREAT-GREAT."

It wasn't actually true, but for once, I thought it was all right to bend the truth a little.

After all, I wouldn't want to hurt anyone's feelings.

I wouldn't want to be like Ms. Lark.

❧

Right before school let out for the day, Mrs. Brisbane gave the class an assignment.

When she said the word "homework," everybody groaned as usual. But my classmates cheered up quite a bit when she told us what it was.

"On Monday, I want you to talk about what you like best about the winter holidays," she said. "We're all going to share our traditions and memories. And if you'd like to bring something in that has a special meaning for you, please do."

There were nods and smiles. Sophie leaned over and whispered something to Phoebe, until Mrs. Brisbane told her to stop talking.

Being a young hamster, I didn't have any traditions.

I'd spent last Chanukah at Stop-Giggling-Gail's house—she's Simon's sister. They lit candles and sang and they opened presents. Oooh, it was wonderful. Then I spent Christmas at Mrs. Brisbane's house and had a hamster-iffic time! They opened presents under a sparkling tree.

But Og didn't come into Room 26 until after the holidays.

"Og, do you know about all the celebrations that happen during the winter break?" I asked him.

He splashed around in the water but he didn't have anything to say.

Poor Og didn't even know about holiday fun.

Suddenly, all I wanted was for my goofy, googly-eyed neighbor to receive a present for the holidays.

And I wanted it to be from me!

HUMPHREY'S WINTER WONDERINGS: I wonder what kind of a gift a frog would like? I do know what a frog's favorite drink is. Croaka-cola!

PRESENTS·PRESENTS·PRESENTS

I wanted to take you home for Christmas, but we're going to my grandparents' farm," Helpful-Holly explained in the car.

It was Friday afternoon and I was on my way to her house for the weekend.

I couldn't see where we were going because her mom put a blanket over my cage so I wouldn't get cold. I tried burrowing under my bedding, but every time the car turned a corner, I slid from one side of the cage to the other.

My tummy felt a little wobbly from all that sliding, and at one point, I got dangerously close to my poo corner—something I try to avoid!

"Why couldn't Humphrey come with us to Grandma and Grandpa's farm?" Holly asked her mom, who was driving.

"I told you, Holly. It's too long a drive for a hamster, especially in the cold," Mrs. Hanson answered. "And Grandma and Grandpa have enough animals on the farm already."

I'd never been on a farm, but I'd heard about them. And I wasn't interested in meeting some of those farm animals, such as large horses and cows and chickens with sharp beaks.

"But they don't have a hamster! And I'd take care of him and make sure nothing happened to him," Holly said.

The car slowed down and then stopped.

My wobbly tummy felt better right away.

"How can I give Humphrey his present when he's somewhere else?" Holly asked. "I was even going to make a little stocking for him."

I thought about that while she carried me to the house. Why would Holly make me *one* stocking when I have *four* paws?

My cage thumped and bumped as Holly carried it into the house. At last, the blanket came off and I realized that my cage was sitting on Holly's desk.

I turned to look around and saw four eyes staring at me!

"Eeek!" I squeaked.

"Billy and Lilly, this is Humphrey," Holly said.

I looked again and saw that the four eyes belonged to two bright orange fish, swimming in a tank on the desk. In the middle of the tank was a bright orange castle.

"Humphrey, these are my goldfish. Do you like them?" Holly asked.

"Yes," I squeaked, and Holly giggled.

I wasn't sure how *much* I liked Billy and Lilly, but I tried to be polite.

"I'm going to do my homework right away," Holly explained. "Then I can spend the rest of the weekend making presents."

"Remember what Mrs. Brisbane said," I squeaked. If only she could understand me!

"She didn't want me to give gifts, but I've already started and I don't want to stop now," she said. "Of course, I can't let you see *your* present, Humphrey," she told me. "I want it to be a surprise."

I like surprises, as long as they're the good kind. And I LOVE-LOVE-LOVE presents! My mind started racing as I tried to imagine what Holly would make for me.

I already knew that Holly was not a lazy human. She was always the first to raise her hand when Mrs. Brisbane asked for a helper.

I'd also noticed that Holly could be a little *too* helpful at times. Mrs. Brisbane's favorite plant died when Holly gave it way too much water, because she thought it would grow more that way. (The poor plant drowned!)

Rolling-Rosie Rodriguez got annoyed because Holly wanted to push her wheelchair when she didn't need help. And Forgetful-Phoebe didn't like it one bit when Holly reminded her of things that she hadn't even forgotten.

I knew Holly meant well. But I didn't know if it was a good idea for her to try to make so many gifts. Especially since Mrs. Brisbane told her to stop.

"See, I have this giant book of holiday crafts." Holly picked up a thick book and opened it. As she thumbed through it, I saw page after page of things to make, with instructions on how to make them.

As she showed me the pictures, she told me about some of the gifts she was planning.

She was making a bookmark for the librarian, and a lanyard for Mrs. Wright's LOUD-LOUD-LOUD whistle. Mrs. Wright is the PE teacher at Longfellow School and as far as I'm concerned, I'd like her better if she didn't have a whistle at all!

"I'm making a calendar to help Phoebe remember dates and this cloth bag for Rosie to hang on the side of her wheelchair to keep things in," she told me. "Oh, and I'm making a miniature garden for Mrs. Brisbane to re-place the plant that died."

Holly's list was so long, I couldn't remember everything she was making. She did say she was making something special for Og's tank, but she didn't say a thing about *my* present.

Then she started snipping and clipping and gluing.

She had music playing in the background, which was nice, until I heard "Jingle Bells" and thought about Joey. I hoped he felt better.

"Holly, don't you want to watch a movie with us?" Mr. Hanson asked when he came in after dinner.

"I need to work on my presents," Holly said. "It's only two weeks until winter break and I have twenty-five presents to make."

"So many?" Mr. Hanson's eyebrows went up. "Who are they for?"

"Everyone in my class," Holly said. "And the teachers and the principal and everyone I know."

Mr. Hanson shook his head. "I don't think everyone in your class will be making a present for you."

"That's fine," Holly said. "I like giving presents. I don't need to get any in return."

"Well, don't stay up too late," her dad said.

After he was gone, I watched Holly cut and paste, color and tape, fold and glue.

She used yarn, cloth, paper and cardboard.

She worked so long, I finally crawled in my sleeping hut and closed my eyes, even though I'm usually wide awake at night.

I must have dozed off, but I woke up when Holly's mom came in and told her she had to go to bed right away.

"It's an hour past your bedtime." Mrs. Hanson turned off the music.

"But all I've made is a bookmark and two snowman finger puppets," Holly complained.

"Holly, you're trying to do too much," her mom said.

"YES-YES-YES," I squeaked. I was getting tired of watching Holly work.

Holly didn't agree. "Mom, it's Christmas and Chanukah and that's when you give presents to people you like, right?"

"Yes, but you could give them each a card," Mrs.

Hanson said. "Now put on your pajamas. You don't want to keep Humphrey awake, do you?"

Mrs. Hanson was a very thoughtful human!

◦~◦

I don't know about Holly, but I was so tired, I fell asleep as soon as she went to bed, until a bright light woke me up.

I crawled out of my sleeping hut and saw that she was busy again, weaving the lanyard for Mrs. Wright's whistle. A flashlight was propped up on the desk.

"Hi, Humphrey," Holly whispered. "I'm going to make a few more presents."

"Okay," I squeaked, although to squeak the truth, I didn't think it was okay for her to do it so late at night.

After all, humans *and* hamsters need plenty of sleep!

I'm not sure about fish, though, because Billy and Lilly always have their eyes (and their mouths) open!

Holly picked up her scissors and cut some paper.

Then she yawned.

Holly picked up a marker and colored the paper.

Then she yawned.

I yawned, too.

She was gluing some yarn on the paper when the door opened and Holly's dad came in.

"Holly, get into bed—now!" he said.

He sounded upset, so Holly didn't argue. She went right back to bed.

"Humphrey, I'm counting on you to make sure she stays in bed," Mr. Hanson told me.

42

"Me?" I squeaked. "I'll try!"

He chuckled and turned off the light.

When he was gone, I kept an eye on Holly. I wasn't sure what I'd do if she tried to get up again, but luckily, she slept soundly the rest of the night.

I guess I did, too, because the next thing I knew, bright sunlight streamed through the window.

HUMPHREY'S WINTER WONDERINGS: How many presents could Billy and Lilly could make? *They* never seem to sleep at all!

A Sweet Idea

Usually when I go home with a classmate for the weekend, we do fun things. But all Holly wanted to do was to work on her presents.

Luckily, on Saturday, her mom insisted that Holly go shopping with her.

Once they were gone and I was sure they weren't coming back for a while, I decided to take a break from my cage.

I was curious about Holly's list of presents.

I was especially curious about one name on the list. A name that starts with *hum* and ends with a *y*.

It didn't take me long to jiggle the lock on my door open. As I strolled across Holly's desktop, I was careful not to knock over any of the jars of glitter or paint or to step on something sharp, like a paper clip or a pair of scissors!

I could feel four eyes following me as I passed by Billy and Lilly. "Don't mind me," I told them. "I'm just looking for the list."

The fishes' mouths opened and closed. It looked as if

they were talking, but there was no sound except the bubbling water. Were they trying to tell me something?

I paused to look at them and they stared back at me and never, ever blinked.

When I have adventures outside of my cage, I try to make sure no one will see me. It felt odd to have Billy and Lilly staring at me. But I was almost pawsitive that they couldn't tell Holly that I'd been out of my cage.

I hurried past the tank and found the list sitting between a box of watercolors and the giant book of crafts.

It was a long list, so I started at the bottom and worked my way up to the top.

Of course, it's not easy for a small hamster to read the huge letters humans write, but Holly's writing was neat and I could make out the names.

Just as she said, there was Mr. Fitch's name with "Bookmark" written after it.

And "Lanyard" with Mrs. Wright's name next to it.

I saw Phoebe's calendar and Rosie's carryall and a few things I didn't know about, such as tissue paper wreaths for some of my friends.

I moved up the list a little more and saw Og's name. Next to it, Holly had written "Mermaid."

Og was getting a mermaid for his tank? Now that *was* a surprise—especially because I didn't think mermaids were real!

I wanted to give Og his first gift, but I didn't think I could come up with anything close to a mermaid.

I was almost to the top of the list, and right above Mrs. Brisbane's name, I saw a great big "HUMPHREY."

But I was unsqueakably disappointed to see this after my name:

????

What kind of a gift is that?

I heard a door slam, so I scurried back to my cage.

When Holly came in, she went straight to work on her presents some more while I watched.

I watched her glue candy canes to a picture frame, which was a useful *and* yummy gift.

Then she made a bookmark with the words "Reading rocks" on it.

By the time her parents told her it was time for bed, she'd checked off quite a few gifts on her list.

But she hadn't crossed off "Mermaid."

And I was pretty sure my name still had those question marks after it.

Holly went to sleep right away. She must have been exhausted from working so hard.

Even in the dark, I could feel Billy and Lilly staring at me and opening and closing their mouths. What were they trying to tell me? I finally crawled into my sleeping hut and after a while, I dozed off.

I had a strange dream about a tiny package sitting in my cage. It had a tiny card that said, "To Humphrey from Holly."

I gnawed off the ribbon and opened the box and in it

was a little carrot. I LOVE-LOVE-LOVE carrots, so I nibbled off a piece. It was yummy. But to my amazement, the carrot suddenly grew bigger!

Since I'm a curious hamster, I took another bite. This time, the carrot grew bigger and bigger until it was bigger than I am!

And it kept on growing and growing. I had to jiggle open the lock-that-doesn't-lock and escape before the giant carrot took over my cage . . . the room . . . and the entire world!

Luckily, I woke up before that happened.

My heart was pounding, but it quieted down when I realized that it was only a dream.

I'd been thinking a lot about Holly's gift to me. But now, I wasn't quite sure I wanted anything more than the peace and quiet of my comfy cage for the holidays.

༺ ⌇ ༻

I guess Holly had finally worn herself out, because the next morning, she slept and slept and slept some more. Finally, her mom and dad came in to see if she was all right.

As soon as Holly woke up, she sat straight up in bed and said, "I've got to get to work!"

"Wait, Holly." Her mom sat on one side of the bed and her dad sat on the other.

"I have to keep going or I won't finish them all!" Holly cried.

"We've got to talk about this," Mrs. Hanson said. "I

called Mrs. Brisbane last evening to ask about gifts and she said she'd already told you there was no gift exchange in your class."

Holly moaned. "But I want everybody to like me!"

"Holly, you don't give presents to get friends," Mr. Hanson said.

"But I want them to know how much I like *them*!"

Then it was really nice, because Holly's mom and dad both hugged her.

I like to see humans hug. (But if a human hugged me, it might hurt a lot! A little stroke of a finger on my back is fine with me.)

"You're trying to do too much and I'm afraid your friends will feel bad because they didn't make a present for you," Mrs. Hanson said. "Did you ever think of that?"

I was truly SORRY-SORRY-SORRY to see Holly's eyes filling with tears.

"She had a suggestion," Mrs. Hanson said. "She said if you wanted to make one gift for the whole class, that would be very nice. And we could donate the presents you've made to children in the hospital. Think how happy they'd be to receive them."

"But what could I make? Everybody is so different. I can't give the whole class one bookmark or picture frame."

"We'll figure something out," Mr. Hanson said. "Now let's have breakfast."

"Pancakes?" Holly asked.

Her mom and dad looked at each other and smiled.

"Pancakes," they both said.

Holly smiled and left the room with her parents.

Which left me alone to think and think and think some more.

What *could* Holly make for the whole class? She was right when she said everybody was different. My classmates were like snowflakes—one present wouldn't fit them all. Or would it?

I decided to check out Holly's great big book while the Hansons were making and eating pancakes. Maybe I could come up with a Plan. I jiggled my lock-that-doesn't-lock and hurried across the desktop.

Then I saw them: Billy and Lilly, swimming around with their wide-open eyes staring at me.

As their mouths opened and closed, opened and closed, I thought maybe they wanted to tell me something. I stopped in front of their tank.

"Hi, Billy. Hi, Lilly," I said. "My name is Humphrey."

They swam. They stared. Their mouths opened and closed. But they still didn't *say* anything.

"Well, nice chatting with you," I said. Then I hurried over to the huge book.

Luckily, it was open. (I'm strong for a hamster, but I might not be strong enough to open such a BIG-BIG-BIG book.)

I glanced at the pages I could see. There were instructions for making a reindeer out of a paper bag, a menorah made of sticks, and a clothespin angel. They were nice ideas, but not quite right for the whole class.

It wasn't easy to turn the page on such a large book, but I found that I could wiggle my nose between the pages, push my head in first and then squeeze in the rest of me. Next, I walked toward the middle of the book and the pages flipped over my head.

I looked at more interesting gifts: a paper cup bell, a stocking made of felt, a thumbprint Santa.

I was about to give up when I turned a page and saw it: the most beautiful house in the world!

It was made of gingerbread, with cake frosting on the roof, a candy cane chimney and yummy candy glued along the sides. The garden was covered with white and fluffy flakes, like snow. (I think they call it coconut.)

I stared and stared at that little house, wishing I had one just like it. All my friends would love a little candy house like that, too.

Then I heard footsteps. I dashed across the desk, past Billy and Lilly, and back to my cage, slamming the door behind me.

I crossed my paws and waited.

Sure enough, Holly went straight to her desk and sat down.

"Humphrey, we didn't think of a single thing that would be nice for the whole class," she said. "What am I going to do?"

"You could look at the picture in the book," I squeaked.

I knew she couldn't understand me, but I wanted to help.

Holly reached her hand toward the book. Yes!

"I've looked through this book a hundred times," Holly said. "There's nothing there." Then she moved her hand and was about to close the book entirely.

"Oh, no!" I squeaked. "PLEASE-PLEASE-PLEASE see that little house!"

I closed my eyes. I couldn't stand to see her miss out on this wonderful idea.

"Wait," she said.

I opened my eyes.

Holly hadn't closed the book. Instead, she was staring at the page with the house.

"Look at this gingerbread house!" she said. "Everybody would like it, don't you think?"

"I sure do!" I told her.

She stared at the page some more. "I love to bake with Mom and Grandma. Mom could help me bake it and I could decorate it."

Holly looked happy for the first time all weekend as she scooped up the book and headed out of the room. "Mom! I just had a *great* idea!" she shouted.

It was nice to see Helpful-Holly smiling.

Even if the great idea was actually mine.

HUMPHREY'S WINTER WONDERINGS: I wonder what it would be like to live in a house made of candy. Or better yet—a house made of carrots. Yum!

In a Spin

"Holly is making a special present for the whole class! And she has two strange goldfish named Billy and Lilly and they live in a tank with a castle!" I told Og when I was back in Room 26 on Monday.

"BOING-BOING!" my friend twanged.

Then the bell rang and class began, so I didn't have time to tell him more.

As usual, Mrs. Brisbane started the day with math.

Then we had a spelling test. I would have gotten 100 percent, except for the word "flurry." I think I had a piece of bedding stuck in my ear because I thought Mrs. Brisbane said "furry." Still, it was my best spelling test of the year!

When it was time for recess, Mrs. Brisbane said it was terribly cold outside, so my friends got to stay inside and decorate the room. They made paper snowflakes, yummy-looking candy canes, and all kinds of funny gingerbread people.

Then everyone gathered in a circle to answer our homework question: What do you like best about the winter holidays?

Thomas was first to shout out, "No school!"

All the rest of my friends shouted "Yes!"

I didn't join in, because school is my home. It's my favorite place.

Unlike my classmates, I also didn't have any idea of where Og and I would be spending the holidays.

Next, Mrs. Brisbane called on Tall-Paul Green.

"Presents!" he answered. "I get a present every night during Chanukah!"

A lot of my classmates said, "Oooh!"

"We light the menorah and add another candle every night for eight nights," he added.

"I like presents, too," Daniel said. "Santa leaves them under our tree."

"I like making presents for other people," Helpful-Holly said.

I certainly knew *that* was true.

"And I help my grandma make cookies when we go to the farm," Holly continued. "I love to help my grandma. I'm making a special present for her."

Mrs. Brisbane smiled. "I guess we all like presents."

Rolling-Rosie raised her hand next. "I like tamales," she said. "My mom and my grandmother—I call her *mi abuela*—and my aunt, Tía Luisa, make one hundred tamales or more. And I help!"

"I love tamales. Tell us more about how you make them," Mrs. Brisbane said.

Rosie nodded. "We put all kinds of yummy things in the *masa*—that's made from corn. Then we roll them up in corn husks and tie them so they can cook. Our whole house smells like tamales. The whole street smells like tamales!"

Just thinking of yummy things wrapped in corn had my whiskers wiggling! I'd love to stay at Rosie's house over the winter break.

"Yum, I can almost taste them," Mrs. Brisbane said.

Sophie's hand was waving wildly, so Mrs. Brisbane called on her next. "I get to set up the little Nativity scene that goes under our tree. The people and the carved animals are tiny, so I have to be careful not to break anything, especially the baby in the manger. See? Here's one of the wise men." Sophie pulled out a small carved figure of a man in robes riding a camel.

"Ooh, and I love the presents and cookies and carol singing, and stockings," she said. "Oh, did I mention the cookies? And the tree!"

It all sounded GREAT-GREAT-GREAT. I would love to see that Nativity scene sometime.

Stop-Talking-Sophie probably could have gone on for quite a while, but Mrs. Brisbane said it was Kelsey's turn to talk.

"My mom and dad took me to see *The Nutcracker* last week," she said. "That's a ballet and I *love* ballet!"

She held up the program with a picture of a little girl dancing on her toes in front of a beautiful Christmas tree.

Mrs. Brisbane asked her to share part of the story with us.

"There's a little girl named Clara. And the dancer was actually a little girl," Kelsey explained. "At midnight on Christmas Eve, all the toys come alive and then mice come in and they get in a big fight. And then there's dancing candy from around the world and—oh, it's hard to explain! But someday, I hope I can dance in *The Nutcracker.*"

She explained it well enough for me to wish I could see *The Nutcracker,* too.

"We celebrate Christmas *and* Kwanzaa," Forgetful-Phoebe said. "Kwanzaa starts on December twenty-sixth. Last year, Mom and Dad and I lit seven candles. Each one represented something important. And we ate fruit and had lots of fun."

I like fruit, so I think I'd like Kwanzaa, too.

"But this year, I'll just be talking to them on the phone," she added. "That's the only present I want."

Phoebe lives with her grandmother while her parents are far away in the military.

I REALLY-REALLY-REALLY hope she gets that call.

"Of course, Phoebe. The holidays are all about family," Mrs. Brisbane said.

"That's what I like," Hurry-Up-Harry Ito said. "Everyone comes to our house. I have six cousins. First we play board games. Then we play Ping-Pong and end up chasing each other all over the house!"

I've seen Harry play Ping-Pong, but I'd like to see him with his cousins—all six of them.

Slow-Down-Simon raised his hand. "I like Chanukah, the way Paul G. does. I like the eight days of presents. I like lighting the menorah. But my favorite part is spinning the dreidel!"

It sounded as if he said "dray-dull." Who would like something dull?

Simon reached in his pocket and pulled out a small wooden top. So that was a dreidel! I'd heard about it last year when Simon's big sister, Gail, took me to their house for Chanukah, but I'd been too far away to see what it looked like! He put it on the table in front of him and made it spin.

I dashed up to the tippy-top of my cage to get a better look.

The dreidel had markings on each of the four sides. "Those are letters from the Hebrew alphabet," Simon said.

He explained that you spin the dreidel and depending on what side it lands on when it stops, you either get money or give up money.

"But it's not real money," he told us. "It's made of chocolate!"

I think chocolate money would taste a lot better than real human money.

Simon let his friends try spinning the dreidel and he even taught them a little song.

"Dreidel, dreidel, dreidel . . . ," everybody sang. I squeaked along.

I was hoping that maybe I'd get to go home with Simon for Chanukah again!

"I like to go caroling," Tell-the-Truth-Thomas said

next. "We go door-to-door around the neighborhood, singing songs. Then everybody comes to our house and we drink hot chocolate. My mom makes the *best* hot chocolate."

This time, I didn't think Thomas was exaggerating at all.

Small-Paul finally spoke up. He said he liked adding things to his elaborate train set to make it look like the holidays.

"I put a pine tree in the middle and decorate it," he said. "And I put candy canes in all the cars. I even put Santa's sleigh with his reindeer on the roof of one of the houses. If you want to see it, come on over," he said. "Just call first."

It sounded wonderful. But I'd had an unsqueakably scary experience on that train, so I didn't mind skipping that one.

Mrs. Brisbane looked at the clock. It was almost lunchtime.

Then she noticed Just-Joey. He was looking down at his feet again.

"How about you, Joey?" she asked. "There must be something you like about the holidays."

Joey looked up. "One year, my dad and I made a regular snowman. Then we made a second snowman, but that one was standing on his head. That was hard to do but it was fun."

"I guess you're hoping it snows this Christmas," Mrs. Brisbane said.

"Not really," Joey answered. "Even if it snows, Dad might not get here this year."

"Oh, dear," Mrs. Brisbane said.

My tail twitched and my whiskers wiggled. I was SORRY-SORRY-SORRY to hear that.

"I'm sorry, Joey. My mom and dad won't be able to come to the Winter Wonderland show, either," Phoebe said. "But my grandmother will be here."

"Well, my mom will be here," Joey said.

I was glad to hear *some* good news.

I crossed all my toes, wishing that Joey's dad would get home for the holidays.

I hoped Phoebe would be back with her family soon.

And I wished with all my heart that it would snow.

(For Joey. As I said, I don't particularly like snow.)

Mrs. Brisbane stood up. But then Holly said, "What do you like about the holidays, Mrs. Brisbane?"

I think our teacher was surprised at first. She hadn't expected to be included.

"Thank you for asking, Holly," she said. "I was a little sad because our son, Jason, and his new wife live too far away to get home this Christmas. But I just found out that my sister is coming to visit. And she's bringing my niece and her husband and their two young children. So I'll also have my great-niece, Jenny, and great-nephew, Todd, for the holidays. I'm looking forward to having a big family celebration."

Early that evening, when Og and I were alone, I looked out of my cage and noticed something sitting nearby.

It was dark outside, but the streetlight lit up our table.

"Look, Og! It's Simon's dreidel," I squeaked. "He must have left it here."

Og splashed noisily in his tank.

I thought about how Simon had spun the dreidel.

Spinning is something I like a lot. I spin on my wheel to pass the time, and it makes me STRONG-STRONG-STRONG. And when I'm rolling across the floor in my hamster ball, it sometimes goes into a spin that makes my tummy do a funny flip-flop.

"I don't think he'd mind if I gave it a spin . . . do you?" I asked my neighbor.

"BOING!" Og agreed.

So I opened the lock-that-doesn't-lock and hurried over to the top. It was about the same size as I was and I saw that the sides were flat.

I got up on my tippy-toes and stood the dreidel up on its spinner.

"Here goes!" I said, and I gave the top a spin.

But—oops—I hung on a little too long. When I finally let go, I was feeling a little dizzy and I tipped over. The dreidel tipped over, too, and landed right on me!

"BOING-BOING-BOING!" Og twanged.

"Don't worry, I'm fine," I said.

I'm not the kind of hamster who gives up easily, so I stood the dreidel up again and gave it a spin. This time, I quickly let go and scrambled out of the way.

It whirled and twirled all around me. In order for me to keep my eyes on it, I had to spin around, too.

"Dreidel, dreidel, dreidel," I squeaked, the way Simon had taught us.

The dreidel slowed, wobbled, then toppled over.

I was about to see what side it landed on when I heard that RATTLE-RATTLE-RATTLE coming down the hall.

"Eeek—it's Aldo!" I scrambled back to my cage and pull the door behind me.

I like Aldo, but I don't want him to find me outside of my cage. A hamster has to have some secrets.

"Greetings, my friends," he said as he turned on the lights.

He pulled his cart into the room and then came over to our table. "How's my favorite hamster and favorite frog tonight?"

"FINE-FINE-FINE," I answered.

Og hopped up and down. "BOING-BOING!"

"What's this?" Aldo asked as he picked up the dreidel. "Oh, I know. Dreidel, dreidel, dreidel," he sang with a smile. "I'd better put this in a safe spot."

He took the dreidel to Mrs. Brisbane's desk, which is a very safe spot.

But before he went to work, he gave the dreidel a

good spin. It was such a good spin, it spun right off the desk and landed on the floor.

I was glad that it hadn't spun onto the floor when I was hanging on to it!

Aldo chuckled and put the dreidel back on the desk.

Later, after Aldo was gone, I looked over at the dreidel.

I love spinning, but I decided to leave it alone for the rest of the night.

⌣⌢⌣

On quiet nights in Room 26, I have a lot of time to think. That night, I thought about what all my friends had shared earlier in the day. I thought Mrs. Brisbane was right when she said the holidays were all about family.

But then I had a truly terrible thought.

I jiggled the lock-that-doesn't-lock on my cage and hurried over to Og's tank.

"Og!" I squeaked. "Remember all those things they said in class about families?"

"BOING-BOING!" he replied.

"But what about us?" I asked. "I don't have a family. I mean, I used to, but I hardly remember them."

I must admit, I do remember the wonderful smell of my mom. And I remember quite a few tiny brothers and sisters. But that's about it.

"BOING-BOING-BOING!" Og twanged in his weird way.

"Oh, no!" I said. It just slipped out. But I suddenly

remembered a lesson on frogs we had long ago, when Og first came to Room 26.

As it turns out, frogs are amphibians. They come out of eggs! So Og probably didn't remember his mom at all. I wondered if he remembered his egg.

Not only that, frogs come out as little tadpoles. They aren't even frogs yet.

I wondered if he remembered being a tadpole.

I stared through the glass at my neighbor, with his green skin, his huge mouth and his googly eyes.

"BOING!" he repeated.

"I know, Og," I said. "It's okay. I'm sure we'll spend the holiday . . . well, I don't know where, but with some family."

He began to splash around in his water.

"Besides," I squeaked softly, "I kind of think that maybe, well, you and I are like a family. Because we live together and we share what goes on here. What do you think?"

Og splashed and splashed and splashed some more.

His splashing made me feel a lot better. It turns out that having a frog in the family is a GREAT-GREAT-GREAT idea!

HUMPHREY'S WINTER WONDERINGS: I wonder if my family ever wonders what happened to me, because sometimes I wonder what happened to them.

Sad Lad, Glad Dad

The next day, after our morning math and vocabulary, Ms. Lark came back to help our class rehearse for the Winter Wonderland program.

First, the girls practiced their snowflake song. They were getting better and better.

Then the boys sang "Jingle Bells." They sounded good! Maybe it was because Joey wasn't singing along. He kept his mouth firmly closed.

"You know, Joey, I miss hearing your voice," Ms. Lark said when the song had finished. "Please join in with the others."

"That's okay," Just-Joey said.

"Well, I want you to," Ms. Lark told him.

"So do I," Mrs. Brisbane said, smiling brightly at Joey.

I was smiling, too. At least I was smiling inside.

The boys sang "Jingle Bells" again. Joey sang along—in a softer voice—but I have to admit, he did sound a little bit like a frog.

Next, Ms. Lark talked about the costumes.

And what costumes they would be!

The girls would wear white shirts. Then they were

going to make big snowflakes to wear on their backs and smaller ones to wear on their wrists. They'd be shiny and glittery and the girls would spin around like falling snowflakes.

The thought of all that spinning made me head straight for my wheel. After all, spinning is something I'm VERY-VERY-VERY good at.

The boys were going to make tails to wear and they'd have bells that would jingle and jangle as they pranced around like horses.

I hopped off my wheel and tried prancing. I'm not sure I looked like a horse, though.

My classmates were as excited as I was about the costumes, and after Ms. Lark left, Mrs. Brisbane had a little trouble getting them to settle down.

But Mrs. Brisbane is such a good teacher, she knew exactly what to do.

She started talking about snowflakes again, and this time, she told us there are seven different types of snowflakes. She showed pictures of interesting shapes and patterns and then my friends got to draw their own snowflakes.

"Og, don't you think snowflakes are beautiful?" I squeaked to my neighbor as the class was busily drawing.

"BOING!" he replied. He dived into the water side of his tank and splashed like crazy.

The bell for lunch break rang and most of my friends hurried out of the classroom.

All except Hurry-Up-Harry. He came over to my cage and said, "Hey, Humphrey, I've got a song for you!" Then he sang, "Jingle bells, your feet smell . . ."

"Hurry-Up-Harry! We've got to get to lunch," Slow-Down-Simon shouted.

"See you later, Humphrey," Harry said.

After he left, I sniffed my paws. Harry was right. My paws smelled like strawberries and carrots and my favorite Nutri-Nibbles. I think they smelled hamster-licious.

～✺～

When I woke up a little later, I heard a voice say, "Are you in there, Humphrey? I can't see you."

I poked my head out of the sleeping hut, but all I could see was a gigantic eyeball!

I didn't dare leave my little house with a thing like that outside.

But then the eye blinked and then a face moved and I could see that the eyeball belonged to Just-Joey.

I scurried out to show him I was there after all.

"Hi, Joey!" I squeaked.

"Oh, there you are," Joey said. "Mrs. Brisbane said I could give you some fresh water."

A giant hand reached in the cage and removed my water bottle. "I'll be right back."

It's a little disturbing when someone removes my water bottle, but so far, no one has ever forgotten to bring it back, not even Forgetful-Phoebe.

Sure enough, Joey quickly returned and put it back in place.

"Here you go, Humphrey," he said. "It's raining, so we couldn't go out for recess."

I looked out of my cage and saw that the rest of the class was busy drawing and cutting things out and talking to each other.

"Mrs. Brisbane said we could work on our costumes for the Winter Wonderland show." Joey sighed. "I wish there wouldn't even be a Winter Wonderland show."

I wiggled my nose. Did he mean that?

"What's the point? I can't even sing because my voice is so bad," he said.

"It's not that bad," I squeaked, but Joey didn't understand.

"Just as well," he said. "My dad doesn't think he's going to be able to come. He lives far away, and he doesn't know if he can get off work on time. And the roads will be bad if it snows."

"Eeek!" I squeaked. I knew that Joey wished he could see his father more.

"Come on, Joey. We've got to work on our tails," Thomas said.

When the break was over, Mrs. Brisbane made my classmates put away their costume pieces and talk about science again.

"It's too bad it's raining and not snowing," she said. "Then we could go out and gather snowflakes and study them."

"Wouldn't they melt right away?" Sophie asked.

"Yes, but I have an idea about that. We would have to look at them quickly," Mrs. Brisbane said.

She went on to explain how snow actually helps crops grow by protecting them from the cold.

It was interesting, but for some reason, I couldn't stop thinking about how the Winter Wonderland program was making everybody feel GOOD-GOOD-GOOD except for Joey.

It was making him feel BAD-BAD-BAD.

When Og and I were alone after school, I was still thinking about the problem. "I think Joey sings fine, don't you?" I said.

"BOING!" Og replied.

"Not like a frog at all," I said. Then I quickly added, "Not that there's anything wrong with the way a frog sings."

Og dived into the water and splashed around.

A little later, Aldo came into the room to clean. He greeted us as usual, then went about his work, dusting and sweeping Room 26.

And, since Aldo is generally a happy human, he even sang a little song about a reindeer with a red nose. *That* would be something to see!

But he didn't talk until it was time for his dinner break.

Then he pulled a chair close to the table by the window where Og and I live and took out his paper bag.

"Well, fellows, the holidays are almost here," he said.

"YES-YES-YES!" I squeaked.

Aldo took a tiny carrot out of his bag and pushed it through the bars of my cage. "Season's greetings," he said.

I didn't say anything, because I was busy chewing my crunchy treat.

"I always love Christmas," Aldo said. "But this year is a special one." Aldo looked at us and smiled a big smile that made his furry mustache look like a half-moon on its side.

"You see, boys, I got some exciting news from Maria," he said. "She's going to have a baby in the coming year. That means we're going to be a real family! I'm going to be a *dad*!"

Aldo's smile just grew and grew!

"That's wonderful!" I shouted, wishing with all my heart that he could understand me. "Isn't it, Og?"

My neighbor was strangely silent.

"Og, didn't you hear that? Aldo and Maria are having a baby!" I repeated.

I guess Og heard me that time because he suddenly leaped up and said, "BOING-BOING-BOING-BOING-BOING!"

That made Aldo's smile even bigger and he let out a loud laugh. "Thank you, fellows," he said. "Your congratulations are appreciated."

Then Aldo took out a huge sandwich and began to eat.

I stopped eating and hid some of the carrot in my cheek pouch.

I wasn't in the mood to eat right then. I was too busy thinking about Aldo and Maria and their baby.

"Yep, next year this time, we'll be celebrating with our own baby," Aldo said. "Isn't that amazing?"

I absolutely, pawsitively thought that it was!

I only wished that Joey could celebrate with his dad *this* year.

HUMPHREY'S WINTER WONDERINGS: I wonder if Aldo's baby will have a mustache like his. If so, I hope it's *not* a girl!

More Sour Notes

O ver the next few days, the most amazing things began to happen.

First of all, large white sheets of cardboard turned into great big snowflakes that the girls could fasten onto their bodies by putting their arms through elastic loops. Smaller snowflakes went onto their wrists like bracelets.

Second, long pieces of colorful yarn were woven together into handsome tails for the boys. They also wore caps with paper ears on them.

By Thursday, the girls learned to swirl around like snowflakes as they sang:

Snowflakes floating through the air
Make a lovely sight.
No two snowflakes are alike,
Almost . . . but not quite.

They looked wonderful, especially Rolling-Rosie, who could spin her wheelchair in perfect circles.

Meanwhile, the boys learned to prance while they sang:

Dashing through the snow,
In a one-horse open sleigh . . .

But there were problems, too. One day, things got WILD-WILD-WILD and Tall-Paul pranced right into Be-Careful-Kelsey, and Forgetful-Phoebe almost knocked Small-Paul over when she swirled out of control.

Just-Joey pranced over to my cage.

"Look, Humphrey—I'm a horse," he said. Then he made a weird noise that sounded a lot like a horse.

"Wheeehngeeeeh!" he said. Or something like that. I think it's called a whinny.

I've never actually seen a horse in real life, but I once saw an amazing movie at Mrs. Brisbane's house that had lots of people riding around on the backs of enormous horses. At least they looked enormous to me.

"Do it again, Joey!" I squeaked.

Guess what? He did! "Wheeehngeeeeh!"

Hurry-Up-Harry and Slow-Down-Simon heard him and rushed right over.

"That was amazing!" Harry said.

"How did you do that?" Simon wanted to know.

Joey did it again.

Harry and Simon tried to whinny, too, but they didn't sound like horses at all.

"Settle down, class. Back to your seats," Ms. Lark said. "Now, girls, you will be decorating your snowflakes with paint first and then glitter. Boys, you need to finish up your ears and tails. I'll bring in jingle bells for you to practice with as well."

All of my friends seemed so excited and pleased. I was, too!

"Daniel, why don't we try the song one time with you playing the 'Jingle Bells' music," Ms. Lark said.

"Now?" Daniel asked.

"Yes, now," Ms. Lark replied.

Daniel shuffled his way to the front of the room where Ms. Lark had her keyboard.

"I'm not used to playing on that," he said.

"I know," Ms. Lark said. "But it's just like a piano. And we'll have a real piano for the show."

She placed the music near the keyboard and Daniel took his place.

"I'll count to four," Ms. Lark said. "On the count of four, you start playing. And remember to follow my direction."

Daniel nodded.

"One, two, three," Ms. Lark counted. "Four!"

I was relieved when Daniel started to play and the boys started to sing, following Ms. Lark's hands as she waved them.

Before long, I realized that something was WRONG-WRONG-WRONG!

The boys sang, "Dashing through the snow, in a one-horse open sleigh . . ."

But by the time they were singing "sleigh," Daniel was still playing the note for "snow."

Not only that, it was the wrong note. It sounded so terrible, my ears twitched and my whiskers wiggled.

"Eeek!" I squeaked. No one could hear me, of course, because there was so much noise.

Ms. Lark kept waving her arms.

"O'er the fields we go," the boys sang.

But Daniel played, "In a one-horse open sleigh."

He hit a couple more clunkers, too. I never knew how bad music sounded if someone hit the wrong notes.

And there was another sound: The girls were giggling.

I couldn't blame them.

Daniel wasn't laughing, though. He turned red and there was a look of panic on his face.

"Stop!" Ms. Lark said.

Daniel froze and everyone stopped singing.

"Sorry, Daniel, but you need to keep up with the boys," Ms. Lark said. "It sounded as if you were performing two different songs."

"They were going too fast," Daniel complained.

"I know it's difficult to play while people sing if you're not used to it," the teacher said. "Have you practiced at home?"

Daniel rubbed his nose. "Sort of," he mumbled.

"I hope you will spend some time practicing this weekend," Ms. Lark said. "We'll try again on Monday."

Daniel shuffled his way back to his chair.

He looked so miserable, the girls stopped giggling.

Ms. Lark left and Mrs. Brisbane took over the class, but Daniel didn't look any happier.

And when they left class for recess, I heard Simon say to Harry, "I hear piano players run in his family."

"Run far away, I hope!" Harry replied with a laugh.

Which was kind of funny, except that it was true.

⁓•⁓

Later in the day, Mrs. Brisbane let my friends work on their costumes. The girls seemed especially excited to make their snowflakes glitter. But before they got started, suddenly Mrs. Wright walked into Room 26.

Mrs. Wright is the PE teacher who always wears a shiny (and loud) whistle around her neck.

She also likes to make sure that everyone at Longfellow School follows the rules.

"Mrs. Brisbane, I want to alert you that there is to be *no glitter* at the Winter Wonderland program," she said.

Some of the girls gasped.

"Oh, no!" Sophie said out loud.

I held my breath as Mrs. Wright put her hand on the whistle. I crossed my paws and hoped she wouldn't blow it, because hamsters have very sensitive ears!

"Oh, but we need it to make our snowflakes sparkle," my teacher said. "We were just about to start."

74

Mrs. Wright shook her head. "I'm sorry, but at our planning meeting, we decided there would be *no glitter*. It's too much extra work for Aldo. And I don't want to find glitter in my gymnasium for the rest of the year!"

"You do have a point," Mrs. Brisbane said. "I certainly don't want to make Aldo's job harder."

Aldo works hard. I know—I watch him every night of the week as he sweeps, dusts and mops our room. I didn't want him to have extra work, either.

But I hated to see the girls looking so unhappy.

"Thank you for your cooperation," Mrs. Wright said. "I'm sure we can have a perfectly nice glitter-free program."

After Mrs. Wright left, the girls all started talking.

"It's not fair!" Be-Careful-Kelsey complained.

"We *need* glitter to make our snowflakes shiny," Rolling-Rosie said.

"*I'll* sweep up the gym," Helpful-Holly said. "I'll make sure there's not one single piece of glitter left behind."

Mrs. Brisbane smiled. "Mrs. Wright has a point. There are other ways to make your snowflakes shiny. I'll think of something. Now . . . back to learning."

The girls didn't seem convinced, but soon, Mrs. Brisbane was talking about something coming up called the winter solstice, which is the shortest day of the year! Since I'm usually wide awake at night, I thought an extra-long night would be FUN-FUN-FUN!

On Friday, the girls were a lot happier as they glued shiny shapes made of tinfoil on their snowflakes. And they were as sparkly as could be.

That afternoon, Do-It-Now-Daniel said, "Humphrey, it's my turn to take you home for the weekend!"

People like Fridays. I guess it's because they have a whole weekend ahead of them. I love Fridays, too, because I get to go home with a classmate and learn something new about humans.

What I don't like about Fridays is having to leave Og behind. He stays alone in Room 26 because he doesn't have to be fed. And transporting his tank is more difficult than carrying my cage.

While Daniel waited for his grandfather to pick him up, I told Og I'd see him soon. "Have a good weekend!" I said.

"BOING-BOING," he answered. It sounded as if he was going to miss me.

Mrs. Brisbane stood looking out the window at the gray sky.

"You know what?" she said.

I wasn't sure who she was talking to, but I squeaked anyway. "What?"

"I'm taking you home for the weekend, Og," she continued. "It feels like snow and I don't want you to get stuck here in case school is closed on Monday."

I guess she remembered the time Og and I got

snowed in. It was SCARY-SCARY-SCARY to be alone at school with no one to feed us or give us water.

I was HAPPY-HAPPY-HAPPY for Og. Now I could enjoy the weekend knowing he'd have fun, too.

After the rest of the class had gone home, Daniel's grandfather arrived.

"Grandpa, meet Humphrey," Daniel said as the old man came in.

Mrs. Brisbane introduced herself to Mr. Popwell, which was Grandpa's real name.

Grandpa Popwell wore a heavy plaid jacket and a funny hat with flaps that came down over his ears.

Maybe those flaps kept him from hearing too well, because he said, "Nice to meet you, Mrs. Bizzbane."

Mrs. Bizzbane—I mean Mrs. Brisbane—helped Grandpa Popwell cover my cage with a blanket and carry it out.

"Bye, Og! Have a great weekend," I squeaked to my friend. I already knew he would, since he was going home with Mrs. Brisbane.

"BOING-BOING!" he answered happily.

"It looks as if we'll have the house to ourselves for a few days," the old man said as we drove away from school. "Your mom has a conference."

"I know," Daniel said. "And Dad's out of town."

"Just you and me," Grandpa said. "The boys."

"Just you and me and Humphrey," Daniel reminded him. "He's a boy, too. But not Lulu. She's a girl."

I heard Grandpa chuckle.

I wasn't sure who Lulu was. Maybe Daniel had a sister.

Once we were at Daniel's house, the blanket came off my cage. Right away, I knew who Lulu was, because she started barking.

That's right—Lulu was a dog and she was barking at *me*!

She was a small dog with curly black fur. But even if she was small for a dog, she was still a lot bigger than I am, and when she barked, I could see some very white, very sharp teeth.

"Settle down, Lulu," Grandpa Popwell told her.

She didn't settle down.

"Lulu, be nice!" Daniel said.

But Lulu wasn't nice.

"I'll put her in the den," Daniel said, and he carried her out of sight, thank goodness.

My heart was still pounding, but once Lulu was gone, I looked around and saw that I was sitting on a table in the living room.

And right across the room was a piano! I certainly hoped that Daniel was planning on practicing all weekend.

Grandpa and Daniel went into the kitchen for a snack, so I scratched around my bedding and found a small piece of broccoli I'd stored there. I like to save bits of food in case some human forgets to feed me—but that hasn't happened yet.

When they came back to the living room, Grandpa said, "Do you have homework to do, Daniel?"

Daniel made a face. "It's Friday! I've been working all week. I'll do it later this weekend. Can we watch TV?"

"Your mother said she didn't want us watching TV all weekend," he said. "Oh, and she said you need to practice piano for the show at school."

"I'll practice," Daniel said.

I was glad to hear that, because from the way he played at rehearsal, he needed *lots* of practice.

"Later," Daniel said.

He said "later" a lot.

"Is it okay if I read for a while?" Daniel asked.

"Sure," his grandfather answered. "And I'll finish that crossword puzzle I started this morning."

I crossed my paws and hoped that when Daniel practiced "later" it wouldn't be too late!

HUMPHREY'S WINTER WONDERINGS: If you say "later" every time you need to do something, do you ever actually get that thing done?

Practice Makes Perfect

When we got to his room, Daniel set my cage on the dresser, pulled a book out of his backpack, then flopped down on his bed to read.

He was quiet for a long time. There wasn't much else to do, so I hopped on my wheel for a spin. That always gets my whiskers wiggling and my tail waggling.

I was concentrating so hard on wiggling and waggling that I almost fell off my wheel when Daniel suddenly said, "Yes!" I thought he was trying to encourage me, so I spun a little faster.

Daniel said, "Way to go!"

"Thanks," I squeaked, though I have to admit I was out of breath.

"Whoa!" he said.

That surprised me so much I stopped spinning completely.

When I looked out, I saw that Daniel wasn't even looking at me. He was still reading his book.

"Humphrey, this book is the best," he said.

Then he finally looked over at me.

"You should read it," he continued.

"I'd like to!" I squeaked.

I meant it, too. I would LOVE-LOVE-LOVE to read more. Does anybody write hamster-sized books?

Daniel sat up and leaned closer to my cage. "See, this boy has a magic backpack and anything he needs comes out of it whenever he needs help. So, there's this part where another boy is bullying him and he reaches into his backpack and pulls out a cream pie! So he throws the pie in the bad guy's face. And when the bully tells the teacher, the pie and the mess magically disappear. I sure wish I had a backpack like that!"

I guess anybody would like that.

"And it can take you places. You put it on and think of a place you want to go and—whoosh—you're there," he said.

That got my brain spinning. I imagined being in my cage and putting on a magic backpack and—whoosh— I'd be on top of Mount Everest (although it would be a little cold there for a hamster). Or I'd be surfing on the Pacific Ocean (although it would be a little wet there for a hamster). I could be on the streets of a big, bustling city (although it would be a little dangerous there for a hamster).

Maybe a magic backpack wasn't such a great idea after all, at least for a small creature like me. But that cream pie sounded YUMMY-YUMMY-YUMMY!

I glanced over at Daniel and could see that his mind was miles away.

"Boy, if I had that magic backpack, when it was time

to practice piano, I could put it on and fly to an amusement park," he said.

"Don't you like playing piano?" I asked, wishing that he could understand.

"I like the piano," Daniel said. "But every time I practice, I make so many mistakes, it sounds awful. That's why I don't like to practice."

I saw his point, but I also thought that if you don't practice something, you'll never, ever get better at it. There was no use trying to explain that to Daniel, though. I knew that all he'd hear would be squeaks.

Daniel stared at the cover of the book. "This D. D. Denby is a genius," he said. "Imagine writing a book like this."

Then he opened the book again and leaned back on his pillow. "I've got to find out what happens next."

Reading is great, but it's not too interesting to *watch* someone read. So I hopped back on my wheel and did some more spinning. I went faster and faster and faster until I suddenly screeched to a stop.

My brain was still spinning, though, because I had an idea. What if there was a story about a hamster who had a magic wheel? He could spin that wheel and go anywhere he wanted! Now, that was a story I'd like to read in a book. I got so caught up thinking about that idea, I didn't notice that it had gotten dark. Daniel had turned on the lamp by his bed.

He suddenly closed the book and sat up. "That's it!" he said. "Finished."

He stared down at the cover. "I sure wish I had a magic backpack to help me get out of playing piano at school," he sighed.

"But you don't!" I squeaked. "So you need to practice."

Daniel read the back of the book's cover. "There are five more magic backpack books," he said. "I hope I get the next one for Christmas."

Just then, Grandpa Popwell came into the room. "It's awfully quiet," he said. "I thought maybe you'd fallen asleep." Then he chuckled. "I guess maybe I dozed off myself. So, how about showing me what a great piano player you are?"

"I'm hungry," Daniel said. "Can we do it later?"

"I'll tell you what," Grandpa said. "You play a song for me now and then we can eat."

Daniel wrinkled his nose. "Just *one* song?"

Grandpa agreed.

They started out the door, but Grandpa came back for my cage. "I bet you don't want to miss this. Do you, Humphrey?" he said.

He was RIGHT-RIGHT-RIGHT. But I was prepared to dive under my bedding if Daniel's playing sounded as terrible as it had at school.

Back in the living room, Grandpa put my cage right on top of the piano so I had a hamster's-eye view of the keys. I was unsqueakably thankful!

Daniel sat down on the piano bench, opened a piece of music and began to play.

I was expecting to hear "Jingle Bells," but instead he played another song. I knew that song, too. It's called "Twinkle, Twinkle, Little Star."

I was sorry that Daniel wasn't practicing "Jingle Bells," but at least he hit the right notes for "Twinkle, Twinkle."

Grandpa clapped when Daniel finished. "Well done," he said. "But wasn't that a song you played when you first started lessons?"

Daniel nodded.

"I'd like to hear one of your new songs. I think your mom said something about you playing 'Jingle Bells,'" his grandfather said.

"But you said I just had to play one song," Daniel told him. "You didn't say which song to play. And I'm *so* hungry!"

"Play it one time through and we'll eat," Grandpa said.

Daniel grumbled under his breath, but he found the music and set it on the piano, right by my cage.

"It's pretty hard," he complained.

"Practice makes perfect," Grandpa said. "Try it."

Daniel tried, I guess.

He even hit *some* of the right notes.

But he hit a lot of wrong notes, too.

When Ms. Lark played "Jingle Bells," I could almost see the prancing horses and a sleigh gliding through the snow.

When Daniel played "Jingle Bells," I could see horses tripping on the snow and a sleigh caught in a snowdrift!

"See? I told you I can't play it," Daniel said when he was finished.

"Sure, you can play it," his grandfather told him. "All you need is practice."

Daniel patted his tummy. "But I'm starving!"

Grandpa chuckled. "Okay. Let's eat."

He and Daniel went into the kitchen, leaving me in my cage on the piano.

While good smells started coming out of the kitchen, I stared down at the keys. I wasn't sure how they worked. There was a piece of paper propped up above the keys. But the paper didn't have words on it—only lines and dots. Somehow, those showed people what keys to push. And when a person pushed the keys, sounds came out.

When Ms. Lark pushed the keys, the music sounded good.

When Daniel pushed the keys, the music sounded bad. At least when he played "Jingle Bells."

I thought of how the song goes. "Jingle bells, jingle bells, jingle all the way."

SQUEAK-SQUEAK SQUEAK. SQUEAK-SQUEAK SQUEAK.

That part didn't seem too difficult, if you could find the right key and hit it three times, then three times again.

And what was the next part? "Jingle all the way."

Or, as I imagined it in my head: SQUEAK-SQUEAK SQUEAK SQUEAK SQUEAK.

That time, you played the same note as the first part once, then three other notes, then ended up on the note where you started!

SQUEAK-SQUEAK SQUEAK SQUEAK SQUEAK. The first note, then a note that was higher, two notes that were lower, then back to the first note.

If only I had a way to get on that keyboard, I thought I could play those notes.

Then I might be the only piano-playing hamster in the world!

But I wouldn't want to get caught out of my cage. For one thing, there was always the possibility that Lulu would get out of the den and come straight for me.

And even if I survived Lulu, there was the possibility that Grandpa Popwell would change my lock-that-doesn't-lock and I'd be stuck in my cage forever!

So I stayed in my cage and thought and thought and thought some more, until I knew "Jingle Bells" so well, it was almost a part of me.

After dinner, Daniel and his grandpa came back in the living room.

"Let's give Lulu a break and take her for a walk," Grandpa said.

That was fine with me, as long as she didn't walk close to my cage!

"Now?" Daniel asked. "It's cold out."

"We'll bundle up," Grandpa said. "Lulu needs the exercise. Come to think of it, so do we, after all that chili."

Soon, Daniel and Grandpa Popwell were wearing coats and hats, gloves and scarves. Then they went into the den and came out with Lulu. Luckily she was on a leash. And she was actually wearing a *sweater,* which seemed strange to me.

She barked at me, of course, but Daniel took her outside while Grandpa locked the front door.

"We'll see you later, Humphrey," he said as they left.

"Bye!" I squeaked back. "Don't hurry back!"

And there I was. No Lulu, no humans, just me and the piano.

HUMPHREY'S WINTER WONDERINGS: I wonder why a dog needs a sweater when she already has a fur coat?

The Keys to Success

I stared down at the keys. There were big shiny white keys. And in between some of them were thinner shiny black keys.

I wondered how long Daniel and his grandfather would be gone. On the one paw, it was cold outside and they might hurry back. On the other paw, it might be the only chance I'd ever have to be alone with a piano, without Lulu around. And I didn't have far to go.

So without hesitation, I jiggled the lock-that-doesn't-lock and slid down onto the keys.

CLANK-CLINK-CLUNK! CLUNKETY-CLINK-CLINK!

When I tumbled down on the keys, the notes sounded even worse than Daniel's playing.

I stopped to get my breath before I looked down at the keys I was standing on.

I remembered that Daniel was playing the keys in the middle of the piano, so I carefully made my way there, note by note.

BING-BANG-BING!

I settled on the middle key and pushed it.

TINKLE!

That didn't sound quite right. I pushed the next key with my paw, but that didn't sound right, either.

JANGLE!

I s-t-r-e-t-c-h-e-d my paw up one more key and pressed it.

JINGLE!

That was it! That was the note where Daniel had begun. (At least he got that part right.) I scurried up to that key to begin and I hit that key three times.

"Jingle bells."

Then I pressed it three times again.

"Jingle bells . . ."

Next came the tricky part. I had to s-t-r-e-t-c-h my paws up, skip the next key and push the one next to that. Then, I quickly turned and s-t-r-e-t-c-h-e-d my paws the other way and pressed the note two keys down from the starting point.

So far, so good. I pressed the next key up and then pressed the key I started with.

"Jingle all the way!" I squeaked.

I'd hit the right notes, but it still sounded wrong. The music was too jerky.

Then I remembered that Grandpa Popwell had said, "Practice makes perfect."

So I played that part again. And again.

The more I practiced, the more it sounded like the way Ms. Lark played it. (Of course, she played with two hands, but I wasn't ready to tackle *that* yet! I do have four paws to work with, but I can only stretch so far.)

It was a GREAT-GREAT-GREAT feeling. In fact, I was having so much fun, I lost track of the time. So I was surprised to hear the door open and footsteps. Daniel, Grandpa and Lulu bounded through the door.

The dog started barking at me right away. I was so shocked, I fell back on the keys with a CLINK-PLINK-PLUNK!

Daniel shouted, "Humphrey's out of his cage!" Grandpa Popwell dragged Lulu off to the den and slammed the door.

"How did he get out?" the old man asked.

Daniel had his hands cupped around me so I wouldn't fall. "I don't know. I checked to make sure the cage was locked."

"Well, put him back in," Grandpa said. "I hate to think what would happen if Lulu got near him."

I hate to think about it even more than Grandpa. I imagine if she got near me, she'd use those sharp teeth in a highly unfriendly way!

Daniel relaxed his hands a bit. "Maybe Humphrey wants to play the piano," he said with a laugh.

"See what he does," Grandpa said. "But keep your hands there so he won't fall. It's a long way down."

"I'll be careful!" I squeaked, which made Daniel and his grandfather chuckle.

I was SORRY-SORRY-SORRY to be caught out of my cage. But at least I had the chance to show Daniel what a little practice can do.

I made sure I started on the right key and played what I'd learned so far.

"Jingle bells, jingle bells, jingle all the way," the notes played.

Daniel gasped. "How did he do that? He played 'Jingle Bells'!"

"It sounded like 'Jingle Bells,' but I'm sure it was a fluke," his grandfather said.

"What's a fluke?" Daniel asked.

"Like an accident. Something that happened by chance," Grandpa Popwell replied.

He thought it was an *accident* that a hamster could play the first part of "Jingle Bells" perfectly? What about "practice makes perfect"?

To prove that it was no fluke, I played the notes again, taking great care to make sure I hit the right keys.

"Wow, that really *was* 'Jingle Bells,'" Daniel said. "Humphrey can play the piano!"

Grandpa looked down at me, shaking his head. "I guess so, but nobody would believe it if we told them. In fact, maybe we should keep quiet about it, so folks don't think we're crazy. But he definitely played 'Jingle Bells.'"

"Play it again, Humphrey," Daniel said.

So I played it again, without any mistakes.

"Grandpa, we should make a show with Humphrey in it," Daniel said. "We could be rich if we had a piano-playing hamster. And Humphrey would be a star!"

Grandpa shook his head. "I don't know," he said. "That would be a lot of work for a little hamster. Humphrey might not like working so hard."

Daniel was disappointed, but I have to admit, my paws were feeling quite sore.

Thank goodness Grandpa told Daniel he'd better put me back in my cage for a rest.

My nice soft bedding felt especially good after scrambling around those hard piano keys.

As I settled in, Daniel said, "If a hamster can play 'Jingle Bells,' then I can, too."

Those words were music to my ears! It was exactly what I was hoping.

Daniel sat right down and practiced playing "Jingle Bells."

The music sounded shaky in the beginning and he hit a lot of wrong notes. But the more he played, the better the music sounded.

After a while, Grandpa said, "Good job!"

Daniel played the song a few more times and Grandpa said, "That sounds great!"

Finally he said, "Daniel, that was perfect!"

Practice makes perfect. I guess it works after all.

That night, I rested quietly in my cage in Daniel's room.

Lulu was in the den with the doors closed, according to Grandpa.

But I kept one eye open all night, just in case.

The next day, Daniel practiced again, with my cage on the piano. He played so well, I could finally see the prancing horses and a sleigh gliding gracefully through the snow!

Late that afternoon, Daniel's mom came home.

"Mom, Humphrey played 'Jingle Bells' on the piano!" he said.

His mom laughed. "Humphrey? The little hamster? That's a good joke."

"Well, he did," Daniel said. "Didn't he, Grandpa?"

Grandpa chuckled. "Yes, he really did."

Daniel opened my cage and took me out. "I'll show you."

He set me on the keys. I stopped and thought for a second.

On the one paw, I was proud to show off what I'd accomplished to help Daniel.

On the other paw, I know Daniel would tell every-one at school what had happened. And he'd said I might become famous as the world's first piano-playing hamster. I might even end up on TV, which would be GREAT-GREAT-GREAT!

But wait. If I became a famous TV star, I wouldn't live in Room 26 anymore. I'd miss my friends and my job as a classroom hamster.

So I made up my mind. I scurried up the keys and then back down.

BING-BANG-CLINK-CLUNK-BANG-BANG-BING!

Daniel's mom laughed. "That doesn't sound like 'Jingle Bells' to me!"

"Play it, Humphrey, please!" Daniel begged me.

I hated to disappoint Daniel, but I also wanted to stay in Room 26, so I scampered up and down the keys again.

CLINK-CLINK-BONG-BANG-CLUNK!

"I should have known better than to leave you two together—making up stories like that," Daniel's mom said. "What I want to hear is *Daniel* playing 'Jingle Bells.'"

And he did.

The third time he played it, his grandpa and mom sang along.

I squeaked right with them.

Later that night, while Daniel was sleeping, I heard Lulu whining outside his bedroom door.

I *almost* felt sorry for her.

After all, she might have sharp little teeth, but I doubt that a dog could ever play the piano. Poor Lulu!

When I got back to Room 26 on Monday morning, I had good news for Og.

"Daniel practiced 'Jingle Bells,' Og. And he's LOTS-LOTS-LOTS better now," I said.

Of course, no one else would find out if he was better until Ms. Lark arrived.

As usual, when my friends came into Room 26, there

a lot of talking and commotion as coats and hats
e hung up and students headed for their desks.

Stop-Talking-Sophie was telling Phoebe and Kelsey
bout the tree her family put up over the weekend.

Small-Paul was showing Tall-Paul a drawing of his
as to expand his train layout.

And over in the corner, Thomas, Harry and Simon
re gathered around Just-Joey.

I couldn't hear what they were saying, but suddenly
et out a loud horse whinny.

heeehngeeeeh!"

et me try," Thomas said. "Weeheenwoooo . . ." I'm
to say that while Joey's whinny sounded like a real
e, Thomas's sounded more like a sick cow.

"My turn!" Simon shouted. He tried to whinny, too.
aaaghaawaagh!" It didn't sound like a horse. More
e a large dog.

"My turn!" Harry said. Unfortunately his whinny
ounded like a cat left out on the porch.

"Wowwwoowowow!"

"Goodness, what's going on over here with you
boys?" Mrs. Brisbane asked as she headed to the corner.

"We're whinnying like horses," Simon said.

Mrs. Brisbane laughed. "Your horses sound as if
they're in pain."

"Not Joey's," Thomas said. "He sounds just like a
horse. Show her." He nudged Joey.

"Wheeehngeeeeh!" Joey whinnied.

He sounded just like a horse.

"That's terrific," Mrs. Brisbane said. "Can you c
again?"

"Wheeehngeeeeh!" Joey repeated.

"You *do* sound like a horse," Mrs. Brisbane said.

"My dad taught me to do it," Joey said.

Mrs. Brisbane seemed excited. "I have an idea! I
going to tell Ms. Lark about this."

The bell rang and Mrs. Brisbane took attendance.

I was unsqueakably excited about what I'd
and seen.

"Og, did you hear it? Did you see what happ
I asked my neighbor.

"BOING-BOING-BOING-BOING!" he answere

Og didn't sound anything like a horse. But he
sound like a very excited frog!

HUMPHREY'S WINTER WONDERINGS: If Og ever played
the piano, would the music make everyone hoppy?

Keep Calm and Focus

"Class, as you know, today we're having a dress rehearsal for the Winter Wonderland show," Mrs. Brisbane said later in the morning.

Dress rehearsal? Not only did I not know we were having one, I didn't know what a dress rehearsal was.

"Ms. Lark will take us into the gym so we can practice onstage. We'll take all our props with us," Mrs. Brisbane explained.

Rolling-Rosie raised her hand. "How can it be a dress rehearsal? We girls aren't wearing white. And we haven't finished decorating our snowflakes."

"I know," Mrs. Brisbane said. "But at least we can try the song on the stage and you can wear your snowflakes as they are. We'll finish decorating them this afternoon. Daniel, are you ready to play the piano?"

Daniel looked pleased as he said, "Yes, Mrs. Brisbane. I practiced this weekend."

"Yes, he did!" I squeaked.

Everybody giggled.

Then Mrs. Brisbane had my classmates line up. They took their snowflakes, bells, tails and ears with them.

Just as she reached to open the door, Forgetful-Phoebe said, "We forgot Humphrey and Og!"

For someone who can be forgetful, Phoebe was good at remembering important things—like us!

"Humphrey and Og are staying here," Mrs. Brisbane told her.

"But . . . then they won't get to see us onstage," Phoebe protested.

Daniel looked truly upset. "I don't know if I can play it without Humphrey," he said. "He helped me play the song!"

"Oh, dear," Mrs. Brisbane said.

"I want Humphrey and Og to see us," Thomas said. "After all, they saw us learn the songs and make our costumes."

"They should be there," Holly added.

Suddenly the class was abuzz with my friends begging Mrs. Brisbane to bring us along.

"But what will we do with them?" Mrs. Brisbane asked.

Daniel had a suggestion. "We can put them on top of the piano. That's where Humphrey was at my house."

"Please! Please!" my friends begged.

Mrs. Brisbane shook her head, which was bad. But then she smiled, which was good.

"Oh, I guess it won't hurt," she said. "But let's be careful with them."

Then she carefully put my cage and Og's tank on a

book cart she keeps in the room. "Who's going to push?" she asked.

Of course, every single student wanted to push.

Mrs. Brisbane chose Phoebe, because it was her idea.

Phoebe gave us a nice easy ride down the hallways of Longfellow School, right past Mr. Morales's office.

He was standing in the doorway as we approached. "Whoa, looks like a parade," he said.

Mr. Morales was wearing a tie with little stars on it.

"We're on our way to dress rehearsal," Mrs. Brisbane explained.

"And what are Humphrey and Og going to do?" he asked.

"They'll be the audience," Sophie said.

Mr. Morales leaned down to look in my cage. "I hope you like the show."

"I'm pawsitive that I will!" I squeaked back.

As we rolled along some more, I heard a familiar voice say, "Hi, Humphrey-Dumpty!" That was A.J., one of my favorite friends from last year's class. He was the first human to give me a nickname.

And then we arrived. The gym is huge! I was only there once before and I hadn't even noticed that there was a stage.

Ms. Lark was waiting there for us. When Phoebe rolled the cart past her, Ms. Lark looked SHOCKED-SHOCKED-SHOCKED.

"What are *they* doing here?" she asked.

"The children wanted to bring them and I thought it couldn't hurt," Mrs. Brisbane replied.

"I don't think it's a good idea." Ms. Lark was looking pale.

"You won't even know they're here," Mrs. Brisbane said.

"Oooh, look at the stage!" Harry shouted.

What a sight! The back wall of the stage was all white with bright green pine trees made out of paper. In front of that was a low fence with snow on top. I guess it wasn't real snow, because it was warm in the gym and snow would melt. But it looked hamster-iffic.

The piano was at one side of the stage. Mrs. Brisbane helped Phoebe put my cage and Og's tank on top.

Ms. Lark's keyboard was on the opposite side of the stage, on a stand.

"All right, class. Let's get organized. Put on your costumes quickly." Ms. Lark looked around nervously.

There was a lot of talking, giggling and jingle-jangling as the girls put on their snowflakes, and the boys held their jingle bells as they put on their tails and ears.

"Take your places!" Ms. Lark said.

It took a while, but they managed to get lined up with the boys on the sides so they couldn't be seen by the audience (there wasn't an audience yet, except for Og and me). The girls lined up in the center of the stage.

"Okay—so first the girls will begin the snowflake song. As soon as they finish, I'll signal you, Daniel. You start playing the introduction to 'Jingle Bells.' Then the boys prance onstage singing," Ms. Lark explained.

"And then the girls will sing a chorus of the snow-flake song while the boys are still singing 'Jingle Bells,'" she said.

It sounded confusing to me, but I knew what Ms. Lark wanted. I only hoped my classmates knew, too.

Ms. Lark stood at the keyboard and raised her hand.

"One, two, three . . . ," Ms. Lark said, and the music began.

Then the most amazing thing happened. The girls twirled around, spinning like snowflakes in a flurry. (That was one of my spelling words, remember?) The tinfoil on their costumes twinkled like stars. Mrs. Brisbane was right—they didn't need glitter!

No two snowflakes are the same,
Though they're lacy white.
No two snowflakes are alike,
Almost . . . but not quite.

Each one is special,
That is true.
Each one is special,
Just like me and you.

Even though they weren't wearing white, I thought the girls looked wonderful whirling like snowflakes across the stage.

"And one, two, three . . . ," Ms. Lark said. "Go, Daniel!"

She pointed at the piano. I saw a look of panic on Daniel's face, so I was relieved when he started to play "Jingle Bells."

With each note he hit, my heart went THUMP-THUMP-THUMP, but I didn't have anything to worry about. This time, Daniel hit all the right notes.

The boys came prancing in from both sides of the stage. Bells were jingling and the boys looked a lot like horses.

I loved it when they started to sing.

Jingle bells, jingle bells, jingle all the way,
Oh, what fun it is to ride in a one-horse open sleigh—ay!

I didn't love it when I noticed that Joey wasn't singing along.

Jingle bells, jingle bells, jingle all the way,
Oh, what fun it is to ride in a one-horse open sleigh!

I have to admit, I wasn't prepared for what happened next. Ms. Lark pointed at Joey.

And Joey let out an earsplitting "Wheeehngeeeeh!"

So *that* was Mrs. Brisbane's idea!

It was a very fine whinny. And he repeated it at the end of the next verse.

The girls started twirling again and sang their

song at the same time the boys sang their song. Instead of sounding mixed-up and confusing, it sounded great!

There were a few *teeny-tiny* problems, though.

The swirling snowflakes got a little carried away. I think Be-Careful-Kelsey imagined that she was dancing in *The Nutcracker* and whirled right into Rolling-Rosie's wheelchair. Rosie spun into Phoebe and, well, let's just say instead of twirling, the snowflakes were stumbling across the stage.

Meanwhile, the boys pranced like frisky horses . . . until Slow-Down-Simon took a wrong turn and the line of boys toppled like a row of falling dominoes!

"Stop!" Ms. Lark shouted.

She stopped playing her keyboard, but Daniel was concentrating so hard on his playing, he didn't even notice. He kept on jingling all the way.

When the jingling-jangling twirling-swirling stumbling-tumbling stopped, Ms. Lark asked, "Is everyone okay?"

My classmates all nodded. That was a big relief!

"You were doing very well," Ms. Lark said. "Just stay calm and focus on what you're doing."

"You can do it!" I squeaked.

"BOING-BOING!" Og agreed.

"Ms. Lark, we'll work really hard," Sophie said. "Won't we, everybody? We did well in rehearsal and our costumes look so good, I know we can do it! I think if we all pull together and—"

"Thank you, Sophie," Ms. Lark interrupted. Not that I blamed her. Sophie did tend to, well, talk a lot!

"Joey, you were great," Ms. Lark said. "You made the song so much better."

Joey's smile filled his whole face.

"We'll practice one more time before the program," Ms. Lark said. "But I need you to *focus*." She added, "Oh, and Sophie, Mrs. Brisbane will talk to you later."

I was a little worried that Sophie was in trouble for talking . . . again.

Then, right before Phoebe wheeled us back to Room 26, Daniel leaned in close to my cage and said, "Thank you, Humphrey."

"You're welcome, Daniel," I squeaked back.

"You're my lucky charm," he said. "You make me play better."

I know he meant it as a compliment, but I wished I could tell him that he didn't need a lucky charm or a magic backpack to play better.

He played better because he practiced!

HUMPHREY'S WINTER WONDERINGS: If a horse lived next door to you, would he be your neigh-bor?

Helping Hands

When Holly arrived the next morning, her dad was with her. And he was carrying a HUGE-HUGE-HUGE box.

Slow-Down-Simon rushed up and asked, "What's that?"

Soon, Holly and Mr. Hanson were surrounded by curious classmates.

"Please, class . . . let Mr. Hanson get through so he can put the box down," Mrs. Brisbane said.

They backed away and Mr. Hanson set the box down on a table that Mrs. Brisbane had cleared for him.

"But what *is* it?" Simon asked.

"It's a present for the whole class," Holly said. "And I made it."

"And we're going to wait until everyone is here before we open it," Mrs. Brisbane said.

Simon and the others groaned. "We'll have to wait forever for Harry!"

Harry and Simon were good friends, but Simon got annoyed when Harry was late, which was often.

All my classmates were eager to find out what was

in the box. Even though I thought I knew what it was, I couldn't wait to see it, either.

Thankfully, by the time the bell rang, Harry was in his chair.

After Mrs. Brisbane took attendance, she said, "Class, Holly has brought something special for everyone. I'll let her tell you about it."

Holly stood next to the box on the table. "I wanted to make each of you a gift to celebrate the season. But I ended up making one gift for the whole class."

"Open it already—please!" Simon said.

Holly carefully lifted the big lid and my classmates gasped. "It's a gingerbread house and I made it myself. Well, with some help from my mom."

"Wow! Can we eat it?" Thomas asked.

Holly looked horrified. "No! Mom sprayed something on it that would keep it from spoiling. It's not good to eat."

"There will be no nibbling, class. Besides, we wouldn't want anything to ruin this beautiful house," Mrs. Brisbane said. "You did a wonderful job."

"Can we see it closer?" Rolling-Rosie asked.

Mrs. Brisbane said that the students could come closer. "But you must be very careful not to touch the house or shake the table."

When they moved up, my friends blocked my view.

"I'd like a better look, too," I squeaked, but I'm sure no one heard me over all the talking.

"BOING!" Og splashed wildly in his tank.

"I want to live there," Kelsey said, leaning in.

"Me too," Tall-Paul agreed.

"It reminds me of the witch's house in 'Hansel and Gretel,'" Phoebe said. "But much nicer."

"There's a card that goes with it," Holly said. "It says, 'To all my friends in Room Twenty-six, from Holly.'"

"Thanks, Holly," Rosie said.

"Thanks!" all my friends chimed in.

"Could you tell us how you made it, Holly?" Mrs. Brisbane asked.

"Og, I wish I could get a better look," I squeaked.

"BOING-BOING-BOING!" Og agreed.

I climbed all the way up to the tippy-top of my cage and got a glimpse of the little house. It looked SWEET-SWEET-SWEET.

"My mom and I made the gingerbread," Holly explained. "Then we cut it in different shapes. We followed a pattern my dad made. Then we put it all together, using icing as the glue."

"Yum!" Rosie said.

"I needed my mom and dad to help with that. Then I put icing on the roof and put cookies on it to look like—what do you call those?"

"Shingles," Mrs. Brisbane said.

"Then I put all kinds of candy all over the house, with candy canes on the chimney and around the door," Holly continued.

"Oh, and there are chocolate drops!" Harry said.

Kelsey pointed to something. "And candy cane trees with gumdrops hanging from them!"

By this time, my friends were leaning over the little house. Mrs. Brisbane asked them to step back and not touch the table.

"After all, Holly worked hard on this," she said.

Everybody moved back while they admired the house.

"I like the licorice stick fence," Small-Paul said.

"I like the cotton candy smoke coming out of the chimney," Phoebe said.

They stood silently for a moment. Then Simon pointed and said, "Oh, look in the window!" He leaned forward and pointed. "A gingerbread man!"

"Where?" my friends shouted.

My whiskers wiggled with excitement.

But my excitement turned to shock when all at once, my friends leaned forward to get a closer look.

"Stop!" Mrs. Brisbane shouted.

But it was too late. The table shook, the little house swayed from one side to the other and then—

CRASH! The gingerbread house collapsed into a heap.

"Og, it's fallen to pieces," I squeaked to my neighbor.

"SCREE-SCREE!" he replied. That's a sound he only makes in case of emergency.

Og was right—this was definitely an emergency.

"Oh, no!" Holly moaned. "No!"

Mrs. Brisbane made everyone stand back. "Stay calm, everyone."

Holly was not calm. Her face was red and tears started running down her face.

"I'm so sorry this happened," Mrs. Brisbane said, giving Holly a hug. "You worked so hard on it. I should only have let one student at a time come up to look."

"I'm sorry, Holly," Rosie said.

"Me too," Thomas added. "It was the most beautiful house on earth."

Small-Paul stepped forward to look at the wreck of a house. "It's broken, but it's not smashed," he said.

"Waaah!" Holly wailed.

Mrs. Brisbane asked Small-Paul what he meant.

"It might be possible to rebuild it," he said.

Holly was sniffling so loudly, I'm not sure she heard him.

"Let's think about it," Mrs. Brisbane said, handing Holly a tissue. "Right now, it's time for math. Please go back to your seats."

Then she began talking about multiplication.

"Doesn't she care?" I asked Og.

"BOING!" Og seemed as surprised as I was.

Tears were still flowing down Holly's cheeks and she began to hiccup. Sometimes it's funny to hear a human hiccup, but this time it wasn't funny at all.

"Holly, why don't you go to the nurse's office and lie down for a while?" Mrs. Brisbane said. "I'll call her and tell her you're on the way."

Holly nodded and left the room, loudly blowing her nose.

Mrs. Brisbane wrote some math problems on the board, but I'm sure my friends weren't paying attention.

"Can't we help her?" Kelsey whispered to Small-Paul. He nodded.

"There must be something we can do," Sophie whispered.

Mrs. Brisbane turned to face the class.

"What's going on?" she said. "This isn't time for talking."

Small-Paul raised his hand. "We'd like to put that house back together," he said.

Everybody agreed. "Yes," they said. "We want to help Holly."

"Me too! Me too!" I squeaked.

Mrs. Brisbane glanced at the clock. "All right, let's try. It's almost time for recess," she said. "Those of you who would like to work on the gingerbread house may stay in. But just this once."

Small-Paul started scribbling on a piece of paper.

The bell for recess rang and guess what?

Everyone in the class decided to stay inside to rebuild the house.

Everyone wanted to help Holly.

Mrs. Brisbane had them gather around the table.

Small-Paul examined the broken pieces. "Luckily, when it collapsed, some of the bigger pieces didn't break," he explained. "So we should be able to glue them back together. Then we can put the candy pieces on again."

"But we don't have that special icing," Rosie said.

"Why don't we use real glue?" Tall-Paul suggested. "We're not going to eat it anyway."

Small-Paul nodded. "And real glue might hold it together better."

They went to work, quickly.

The two Pauls and Mrs. Brisbane got the walls back up again and glued them.

Kelsey and Phoebe put on the cookie roof.

Thomas and Joey rebuilt the licorice fence.

Rosie pieced the gingerbread man back together again.

Then the rest of my friends helped glue the candy back on.

Everybody helped. I wished I could help, too. At least I could encourage my friends. "Good job!" I shouted.

"BOING-BOING!" Og twanged.

They were almost finished when the door swung open and Mrs. Wright walked in. She was bundled up in a thick jacket and had a scarf wrapped around her neck.

But I could still see her whistle hanging from her neck.

"Mrs. Brisbane, what are your students doing inside? You know they're supposed to go out for recess," she said. "The rules say—"

Mrs. Brisbane is usually polite, but this time she interrupted Mrs. Wright.

"I know about the rules," she said. "But we had an emergency in the class."

She explained about the gingerbread house, the accident, and how upset Holly was.

"I think we can break the rules just this once so my students can help a friend who's in pain, don't you?" Mrs. Brisbane smiled.

I could see that Mrs. Wright was surprised, but then she shocked me.

"I think so," she said. She looked at her watch. "You'd better get back to work. Recess will be over soon."

And she left without blowing her whistle even once.

By the time the bell rang, the house was put back together again.

To squeak the truth, it didn't look quite the same. Even from my cage, I could see that it was a little crooked.

But it didn't matter. What mattered was that the whole class had worked together to help Holly.

A few minutes after my classmates were back in their seats, the door opened and Holly came in. Her eyes were red, but she wasn't crying anymore.

"Welcome back," Mrs. Brisbane said with a smile. "We have a little surprise for you." She pointed at the gingerbread house.

Holly's eyes were wide as she hurried to the table. "But who? I mean what? I mean . . ."

I don't think Holly knew what she meant.

"All your classmates wanted to help you, Holly. So

during recess, they put the house back together," Mrs. Brisbane explained.

Holly stared down at the little house. I was afraid she was going to cry again.

But instead, she smiled!

"You did this . . . to help me?" she said, turning to the class.

"Sure, Holly," Kelsey said. "You're always helping us."

All my friends were smiling and nodding, including me.

"You gave your friends a gift," Mrs. Brisbane said. "And they gave you a gift back."

"Thank you," Holly said.

I had a warm feeling from the ends of my whiskers to the tip of my tail.

HUMPHREY'S WINTER WONDERINGS: I wonder if a gingerbread man puts a cookie sheet on his bed.

The Perfect Present

On Thursday afternoon, things suddenly changed. "Oh, my gosh—look!" Thomas shouted. "It's snowing!"

I turned and looked out the window behind me. Big, thick snowflakes were tumbling down from the sky.

My friends ooh-ed and ahh-ed and Mrs. Brisbane told them they could come to the window and look out.

"Do you think any two of them are the same?" Phoebe wondered aloud.

"Our experiment!" Small-Paul said. "You said if it snowed we could study the snowflakes."

"That's right!" Mrs. Brisbane said.

Then, so many things happened. Mrs. Brisbane sent Paul F. (that's Small-Paul) down to the office to ask someone in the principal's office to get something from the freezer. She and my classmates got their coats on and then Mrs. Brisbane took a magnifying glass out of her desk drawer.

Small-Paul came back with a package of black paper that Mrs. Brisbane had frozen. (Humans are strange, you know.)

Mrs. Brisbane handed Paul his coat and then they all raced outside.

Suddenly, it was QUIET-QUIET-QUIET in Room 26.

"Og?" I asked. "Do you know what happened?"

My froggy friend didn't answer. He only splashed around in the water.

Then I saw them out my window. They were catching snowflakes on pieces of black paper, then bending over them with the magnifying glass.

"They're looking at snowflakes," I told Og. "I hope they'll tell us about it," I said.

"BOING-BOING," Og replied.

And guess what? When they were back in the classroom, they did!

"The paper had to be frozen ahead of time so the snowflakes wouldn't melt right away," Mrs. Brisbane said. "So what did you see?"

"There were about a million broken snowflakes," Thomas T. True answered.

Thomas does like to exaggerate.

"A lot of them were broken," Mrs. Brisbane said. "But how many of you saw snowflakes with six sides?"

All my friends' hands were raised.

"And they were all different," Sophie said. "No two were alike. So maybe Paul F. was wrong about that."

"You'd have to look at trillions of snowflakes to know," Paul replied.

"They were beautiful," Rolling-Rosie said.

Mrs. Brisbane let my friends take time to draw the types of snowflakes they'd seen.

While they worked, she called Sophie up to her desk and talked to her so softly, I couldn't hear a word they said.

At first, I thought Sophie was in trouble for talking too much, again. She loves to talk!

But when I saw her smile, I knew she couldn't be in trouble.

So what was Mrs. Brisbane telling her?

Sophie nodded and then nodded again.

Mrs. Brisbane took a piece of paper out of her drawer and handed it to her.

I was only sorry Mrs. Brisbane forgot to tell me what was going on. After all, I am the classroom pet!

❦

It had been an exciting day in Room 26! I was staring out the window, trying to get a good look at the falling snowflakes, but I guess I dozed off. I woke with a start when I heard Mrs. Brisbane say, "So, class, tomorrow is the big day. We'll rehearse the songs in the classroom before the show. After Winter Wonderland is over, you'll go home with your families for the winter holidays."

Tomorrow! I couldn't believe my tiny ears.

I wish I had a tiny calendar hidden behind my mirror, along with my notebook.

"Don't forget to practice tonight, Daniel," Mrs. Brisbane said as my friends left for the day. "You too, Sophie."

I knew Daniel would be playing "Jingle Bells," but I had no idea what Sophie would be practicing.

And I still had no idea where I would be spending the winter break.

Everybody in the class would be celebrating, but what about Og and me? Would we have anything to celebrate?

Og! I suddenly realized that I hadn't been thinking enough about my next-door neighbor. I wanted to give him a gift . . . but so far, I hadn't done anything about it.

It's not easy to think of a gift for Og.

For one thing, he's always splashing around in water, so he'd ruin just about anything.

For another thing, he's always watching me. He never closes his eyes (that I've seen). So if I wanted to make him something, he'd see me and it wouldn't be a surprise.

Besides, what do frogs like except flies and crickets and other icky things to eat?

Thinking about what Og liked to eat gave me an idea.

If I could only think of a way to distract him.

I pulled out my notebook and began to make a Plan.

⁓

After school, while it was still light out, I decided to put my Plan to work.

I jiggled the lock-that-doesn't-lock on my cage and scurried over to Og's cage.

"Og, there's something I need to do, but I'm worried

117

that Aldo will come in and find me," I said. "Could you watch the clock for me and warn me if it's time for him to clean?"

I don't know if Og can read or write. But in the past, he has often warned me about things, particularly when I've lost track of time. So he must know something about clocks.

"BOING!" Og hopped up onto the land part of his tank and faced the front of the room where the big clock is located.

Hooray—he understood!

I darted behind his tank and raced over to the corner where our food is stored.

While I looked longingly at my beloved Nutri-Nibbles, Mighty Mealworms, Veggie Dots and Hamster Chew-Chews, I passed right by. I glanced at the can of crickets—EWWW!—then headed for the jar of Froggy Food Sticks.

The small sticks were perfect for what I wanted to do. But how was a small hamster going to get them out of a plastic container with a lid?

Luckily, when I was making my Plan, I thought about this.

I took a run at the container and managed to knock it on its side. (I almost got knocked on my side, too!)

I went up to the plastic cap and tapped it. Just as I feared, it was fastened tightly.

However, I'm VERY-VERY-VERY strong for a VERY-VERY-VERY small creature.

So I stood on my back legs and put both front paws against the lid and pulled.

The edge only bent back a little, so I tried again, pulling even harder. "Ooof!"

But it still didn't come off.

I don't give up easily, so I looked around. Lying on our table, not too far from my cage, was a pencil. I hurried over and rolled the pencil up to the Froggy Food Sticks.

"Keep your eyes on that clock!" I told Og.

"BOING-BOING!" he replied.

I held the pencil with both of my front paws, put the pointed tip under the edge of the lid and gave it one big push. All at once, the lid popped off and a pile of Froggy Food Sticks tumbled toward me.

Ewww! My whiskers wilted as the sticks gave off a smell like stinky fish. But this was a gift for Og, after all. He *loves* stinky stuff.

"Everything all right, Oggy?" I squeaked.

"BOING!" he said.

It would take too long to carry the sticks to the side of Og's tank. I had a better idea. I stood up on two feet and pushed the pile with my front paws, moving them in the direction of his tank.

Then I did it again and again, until I had a nice pile of Froggy Food Sticks in place. Luckily, Og was still looking toward the clock.

"I won't be long now," I told him.

"BOING-BOING," Og twanged.

Since I had it all planned out, it didn't take long for me to use my nose and paws to arrange the sticks in the shape of a Christmas tree.

I wasn't sure I'd ever get the smell of stinky fish off my paws, but after all, you shouldn't be selfish if you're giving a gift.

Then I scurried back to my cage and tore out a page of my notebook where I'd made a little card for Og earlier in the afternoon.

I had a little trouble with the card. I started out writing "Happy Chanukah," but I didn't know how to spell "Chanukah," so all I'd written was "Happy."

Then I'd tried to write "Merry Christmas," but I didn't know how to spell "Christmas," so all I'd written was "Merry."

I'd been in a BIG-BIG-BIG hurry at that point, so I'd written, "Frog."

That's all I had time to write. It wasn't much of a holiday greeting, but it would have to do.

"Og, could you come over to my side of the tank now? I have something for you," I said.

Then I scampered back to my cage.

It took Og a while to move from one side of the tank to the other. I think he liked looking at the clock.

But when he finally saw the food stick tree and the note, he said, "BOING!"

"It's a present from me, Og. It's a Christmas tree with a note that says, 'Happy Merry Frog.' Oops, I forgot to sign my name," I explained. "I hope you like it."

Og stared and stared at the tree and the note with those bulging eyes of his.

I was afraid he had no idea what I was talking about.

Then all of a sudden, he started hopping up and down, up and down, crying, "BOING-BOING-BOING-BOING!"

He liked it!

Og kept hopping and BOING-ing.

He was a very happy and merry frog.

I was feeling happy and merry myself.

᠃⟞᠃

I was resting comfortably in my cage when I heard Aldo approaching.

RATTLE-RATTLE-RATTLE! I think the wheels of his cart needed oiling.

The door opened and there he was!

"Hello, my friends!" Aldo shouted as he came into Room 26. "Season's greetings!"

"Hello, Aldo!" I squeaked.

Og splashed around in his tank.

"How do you like the snow?" Aldo said. "Hey, what do snowmen wear on their heads?"

I thought and thought, but I had no answer.

"Snow caps!" Aldo replied. And he laughed and laughed and laughed.

I laughed, too.

Aldo went right to work, cleaning our classroom.

"Say, fellows, I was happy to find out that they decided there would be no glitter at the show tomorrow," he said. "You've got glitter once, you've got it forever. I've swept up pieces of glitter that have been hiding for years."

"Then I'm glad, too, Aldo!" I said. When Mrs. Wright had first said our class couldn't use glitter, I was upset with her. But I decided that this time, Mrs. Wright was right.

"After all, I want to get home after the show and be with Mama Maria," he said. "I've got to start thinking about being a dad."

I was sure that Aldo will be a great dad.

He's already a great cleaner, a great student, and an unsqueakably great friend.

Aldo dusted and swept all the tables in the room until he finally came to our table.

"What's this?" he asked as he looked down at the Froggy Food Sticks tree. "It's a little Christmas tree!"

Then he laughed until his mustache wobbled. "And a little card. 'Happy Merry Frog,'" he read. "I guess somebody in this class likes you, Og. What am I saying? *Everybody* likes you and your friend Humphrey."

"BOING-BOING!" Og agreed.

"But you haven't gotten to enjoy your present yet," Aldo said. "Here . . . open wide." He scooped up a handful of the Froggy Food Sticks and threw them into Og's tank.

"BOING-BOING-BOING-BOING-BOING!" Og said as he opened his huge mouth wide to catch them all.

Aldo laughed some more as he watched my friend.

"I think somebody gave you the best present in the world," he said. "Right, Og?"

Og splashed and splashed until drops of water spilled over the top of the tank.

Aldo was still laughing as he sat down to eat his dinner. "Tomorrow's the show," he said. "So if I don't see you after that, I wish you both the happiest holidays ever. Whatever you celebrate, may you celebrate it well."

"I wish that for you, too, Aldo!" I squeaked with great excitement. "And for Maria and the baby. And for everybody!"

Aldo chuckled. "Humphrey, there's nobody like you."

I certainly hope not! Maybe there are two snowflakes alike somewhere, but there are no two humans who are alike.

And I'm pretty sure no two hamsters are alike, either!

◦•⌣•◦

Nights are long in the winter, and if you're a wide-awake hamster, they seem to go on forever. On Thursday night after Aldo left, I spun on my wheel, climbed my tree branch, made a trip to my poo corner, rummaged around for food . . . and it was still early.

I sat in my cage, looking out at the classroom lit by the streetlamp outside the window.

"Og," I squeaked. "Isn't Holly's gingerbread house the most wonderful thing you've ever seen?"

Og splashed around, but he didn't seem too

interested. I guess if the house had been made of crickets or something stinky, he would have liked it more.

"Have you noticed that it's just my size?" I asked.

Og was quiet, so I guess he hadn't noticed.

I continued. "Holly will probably take it home for the holidays. I was just thinking that I might go over and have a peek at it while I have a chance."

"BOING-BOING-BOING!" Og sounded worried.

"Oh, I'll be careful," I told him as I jiggled the lock-that-doesn't-lock and scurried out of my cage.

I slid down our table leg and hurried over to the bigger table where the gingerbread house sat. The table is next to a reading area where Mrs. Brisbane keeps a tall wire rack full of books. If my friends have free time, they can pick out a book to read or check it out and take it home.

The book rack reminded me of my climbing ladder, so I knew what to do. Very carefully, I pulled myself up from one wire to the next until I was on the same level as the gingerbread house.

As I climbed, I saw some unsqueakably interesting book covers. One showed a dinosaur with huge teeth. I hurried past that one. But there was another one with a mouse wearing knight's armor, standing in front of a castle. I hope Mrs. Brisbane will read that one to the class someday.

I hopped onto the table and there it was: the gingerbread house, covered in the most yummy-looking candy I'd ever seen!

"BOING-BOING!" Og warned.

I'm glad he did, because I was just thinking that no one would notice if I took a teeny bite of a candy cane or a nibble of a gumdrop.

"BOING-BOING-BOING-BOING!"

I almost thought Og could read my mind. But he was right. Holly had said that her mom had sprayed something on the house and no one should eat it.

"All right, Og! I won't take a bite," I squeaked.

As I inched closer, I noticed that instead of smelling like sweet, delicious candy and cake, the gingerbread house smelled like something Aldo used to mop the floor. And it was a lot shinier than cookies usually looked.

The smell was strong, so I held my breath and gazed at the licorice stick fence and the candy cane chimney with the cotton candy smoke. I took another breath and held it just long enough to peek in the windows of the house and see the gingerbread man inside. He gave me a jolly smile.

I felt a little dizzy, so I gave the gingerbread house one more look, then scampered back to the book rack and made my way to the floor.

When I returned to our table, I grabbed on to the blinds cord, as usual, swung my way back up, then let go and leaped onto the tabletop.

(I have to be VERY-VERY-VERY careful with the timing of that move.)

As I passed by Og's cage, I said, "Thanks for reminding

me that just because something looks tasty, it doesn't mean it's good to eat!"

"BOING-BOING-BOING!" he agreed.

Back in my cage, I wondered about what I'd said. If something *doesn't* look tasty—like an icky insect—is it possible that it still could be good to eat? Og certainly thought so. But I wasn't about to try a diet of flies and crickets and Froggy Food Sticks . . . ewww!

HUMPHREY'S WINTER WONDERINGS: If I got a present and Og did not, would he be green with envy?

On with the Snow

The day of the show was also the last day of school. My friends were full of energy, but Mrs. Brisbane calmed them down and they finished up their school-work.

In the afternoon, Ms. Lark came to the classroom to wish us luck.

"I know you'll do a great job this evening," she said. "Remember, keep calm and stay focused. Daniel, you'll practice again after school?"

He nodded.

"Sophie, you know what you're doing?" she asked.

Sophie nodded.

I was glad she knew what she was doing, because I certainly didn't.

Ms. Lark continued, "You'll meet here and get in your costumes. Then ten minutes before you go on, I'll stop by to help you line up and walk to the gymnasium."

Mrs. Brisbane thanked her and we went on with the rest of the day.

When class was almost over, Mrs. Brisbane let my friends practice the songs while sitting in their seats.

It sounded so good, I was SURE-SURE-SURE it was going to be a great show!

Then Holly raised her hand and asked who would be taking Og and me for the holidays.

My ears perked up because it was something I'd wondered for a long time.

Mrs. Brisbane smiled and said, "I guess it's selfish of me, but I'm taking them both home. I want Todd and Jenny to get to know them. Besides, you'll all be busy building snowmen, because I heard on the radio that it's supposed to snow late tonight."

My friends seemed pleased to hear about the snow, except for Joey.

He looked at the window and then he closed his eyes for a second.

I knew he was wishing that his dad could make it home before the snow arrived.

When the bell rang at the end of the day, everyone raced out of the room, except for Mrs. Brisbane.

"I think I'll leave you two here for now," she said. "I'll pick you up after the show."

"GOOD-GOOD-GOOD," I said. "Because I want to be here to see my friends."

Mrs. Brisbane chuckled. "I guess you're as excited as the rest of the class."

She was right!

꙳

It was dark when everyone returned to Room 26.

"Aren't you excited, Og?" I squeaked.

"BOING-BOING!" He dived into the water side of his tank and splashed around.

Mrs. Brisbane arrived first with her husband, Bert.

He rolled his wheelchair over to our table. "So, I hear you guys are coming to visit," he said. "That's enough of a present for me!"

"Me too!" I agreed.

The girls were all dressed in white shirts and black pants or skirts. Mrs. Brisbane helped them get their snowflakes on their backs and wrists.

They were shiny and shimmering and no two were alike.

The boys wore dark shirts and pants. Mr. Brisbane helped them with their tails and ears. Once they had their bells, the room was jingling and jangling like mad!

In fact, everybody was talking and laughing.

Rosie showed Mr. Brisbane how to twirl like a snowflake in his wheelchair.

I heard Phoebe tell Kelsey that she was so excited because her grandmother was recording the show so her parents could see it.

Sophie was talking and talking . . . to herself this time!

And Joey was practicing his whinny. "Wheeehn-geeeeh!"

"Students, why don't we start to line up now?" Mrs. Brisbane said. "Ms. Lark will be here soon."

While she helped them start a line, Daniel came over

to my cage. "Okay, Humphrey. I need you to bring me good luck again."

He picked up my cage and moved toward the line.

"What about Og?" I squeaked. But just then, Daniel tilted the cage and I slid all the way across. "Eeek!"

"Aren't we taking Og?" Phoebe asked Daniel.

He shrugged. "I don't know."

The door opened and Ms. Lark came in. I couldn't get a good look at her from my cage, but I heard her tell everyone how great they looked.

The line started to move into the hallway. Suddenly, Ms. Lark said, "What are you doing with that cage?"

Daniel said, "I'm taking Humphrey. He's my good-luck charm."

Then I could see her. Ms. Lark wasn't tall, but as I looked up at her from my cage, I saw a giant face. A giant, no-nonsense face.

"There is no way you're taking that creature into the gym," she said.

"But I need him for luck," Daniel said. "I can't play without him."

"Put him back," she demanded.

"But you let him come the other day . . . ," he began.

"Against my better judgment," Ms. Lark told him. "Put him back *now*."

"Yes, Daniel. I know you'll be fine without him," Mrs. Brisbane said.

Daniel carried my cage back and set it on the table by the window. "I can't play it without you," he said.

"Yes, you can!" I squeaked, even though I was disappointed I'd miss the show.

Suddenly, Daniel opened the door to my cage and scooped me up. "Come on, Humphrey. No one will know."

And he put me in his pocket, which was down near his knee.

A pocket isn't a good place to put a hamster.

The bad news was that it was dark and hot in there. The good news was that I was going to the show after all!

"Bye, Og!" I yelled, though I'm sure he couldn't hear me.

BUMP-BUMP-BUMP, BUMP-BUMP-BUMP. The class headed down the hall.

Once the bumping stopped, I knew we were somewhere near the gymnasium.

"Hey, we can see the stage from here," I heard Daniel tell Thomas.

"Wow—it's all snowy," Thomas replied.

I used my paws to climb up the inside of the pocket and poked my head out of the top.

We were standing in the hallway, but I could see the stage from an open door into the gym.

The students from Miss Loomis's class were onstage, wearing bright sweaters, scarves and earmuffs, and singing about a winter wonderland.

I recognized some of them from my class last year: Golden-Miranda and Speak-Up-Sayeh, Wait-for-the-

Bell-Garth and Sit-Still-Seth. And they were all gathered around a great big snowman!

"Eeek!" I squeaked. "He'll melt!"

Daniel pushed me back down into the pocket and I couldn't see anything. I did sniff out two raisins stuck to the cloth. They were squashed but still tasty.

After a while, we started moving again. I could feel us moving up some steps and then up onto the stage.

THUMP! That was Daniel sitting down on the piano bench.

"Now Mrs. Brisbane's class will perform for you. But first, an introduction from Sophie Kaminski."

I peeked out of the pocket again. Sophie walked to the center of the stage and faced the audience. She wasn't wearing her snowflake costume.

The audience! I turned and saw them: mothers and fathers, sisters and brothers, grandmothers and grandfathers and lots of friends. The gymnasium was packed with people.

Sophie stared out at the crowd. Everyone waited for her to say something, but for the first time ever, Stop-Talking-Sophie didn't seem to feel like talking.

I wished I could tell her to squeak up!

Luckily, Mrs. Brisbane cleared her throat loudly.

Sophie suddenly opened her mouth and said, "Most people think that no two snowflakes are identical. However, scientists aren't sure. Just for tonight, we'll say that no two snowflakes are the same, because in our class, no two students are the same. And we're happy about that!"

Then she walked to the side of the stage and Mrs. Brisbane helped her put on her snowflakes.

"One, two, three, four . . . ," Ms. Lark said.

The music began to play and the girls came twirling and whirling and sparkling onstage, singing their song.

No two snowflakes are the same . . .

People were ooh-ing and ahh-ing at the lovely sight.

When they finished, Ms. Lark pointed to Daniel, and he began to play as the boys came onstage, prancing and shaking bells and singing with all their hearts.

Jingle bells, jingle bells, jingle all the way,
Oh, what fun it is to ride in a one-horse open sleigh— ay!
Jingle bells, jingle bells, jingle all the way,
Oh, what fun it is to ride in a one-horse open sleigh!

Just-Joey let out a fine "Wheeehngeeeeh!" and the audience roared with laughter.

Every single time Joey whinnied, the crowd reacted happily.

Then the girls whirled in again and sang their snow-flake song while the boys sang "Jingle Bells."

It sounded so good, I had to have a better look, so I pulled myself UP-UP-UP—and then something terrible happened.

I started falling DOWN-DOWN-DOWN!

I had to stop myself, so I grabbed on to Daniel's pant

leg. He kept playing, but some of the notes he hit weren't quite right.

I was barely listening, though, because I started sliding DOWN-DOWN-DOWN.

Whew! I made it safely to the floor. I was going to try to get safely behind the piano, but as soon as I turned, Be-Careful-Kelsey twirled right toward me.

I darted away, just as Rolling-Rosie whirled dangerously close to me.

I took a sharp right turn and here came the horses, jingling and jangling so close, one of them almost pranced on my tail.

"Humphrey!" I heard Harry exclaim.

"Humphrey!" other friends shouted.

There was a stir in the audience, but I wasn't bothered by that.

I was bothered by the fact that my friends were all whirling and prancing to avoid stepping on me, which meant they were crashing into one another.

Then I heard a sound unlike anything I've ever heard before.

"Eeeeeeeek!" someone was screaming. "Eeeeeek!"

I didn't know a human could make such a loud sound.

Everybody stopped to look in the direction of the "Eeeeeek!"

It was Ms. Lark. She was standing on a stool and screaming. "Get it out! Get it out!"

And then the thing I always dread happened. Mrs. Wright blew her whistle.

SCREEEECH!

I was jittery enough as it was, but that shrill blast almost made me jump out of my fur coat!

"Everyone stop where you are!" she shouted.

I stopped. The music stopped. The whirling and twirling and prancing stopped.

Even Ms. Lark stopped screaming.

Mrs. Brisbane ran onto the stage, gently picked me up and held me in the palm of her hand. I was trembling from all the excitement (*and* the whistle), but she stroked my back with her finger and that calmed me down.

She stepped to the front of the stage and spoke to the audience.

"Families and friends," she said. "Some of you may not have met Humphrey the Hamster. He's the classroom pet in Room Twenty-six and we all love him. I don't know how he got in here . . ." She shot a knowing look in Daniel's direction. "But everyone seems to be safe and sound. So do you think we should try the number again?"

The audience cheered and clapped.

Someone yelled, "Encore," which I think means "some more."

Mrs. Brisbane carefully handed me to Joey. "Don't take your eyes off him," she said.

"I won't," Joey promised. He also gave my back a soft and reassuring rub.

Mrs. Brisbane helped Ms. Lark off her chair. She still looked a little shaky, but she went over to her keyboard.

Mrs. Brisbane got everyone back in place, took me back from Joey and moved to the far side of the stage.

"One, two, three . . . ," Ms. Lark began again.

I carefully peeked over the edge of Mrs. Brisbane's hand and I was amazed at what I saw and heard!

Every note was perfect. Every prance and whinny, every jingle and jangle, every whirl and twirl was wonderful.

Until all of a sudden:

"Wheeeh—!" Joey stopped in the middle of a whinny. He was staring at the door.

I twisted my head to look. A tall man with a bright red cap was standing in the doorway, smiling. He took off his cap and waved it.

I looked back at Joey. He was waving, too.

His great big smile let me know that the man was Joey's dad. He'd made it!

Then Joey opened his mouth wide and let out his biggest whinny yet. "Wheeehngeeeeh!"

When the number was finished, the audience stood up and applauded.

Ms. Lark made my friends take a bow.

"Bravo!" the crowd shouted.

"Bravo!" I squeaked. I wasn't exactly sure what it meant, but I knew it was something good!

Our class left the stage and Mrs. Brisbane rushed me back to Room 26 and my cozy cage.

"Humphrey, I don't know how that happened, but please don't ever do that again. I almost fainted!" she said.

"Me too! Me too!" I squeaked.

"BOING-BOING-BOING!" Og twanged.

"Don't worry, Og. I'll tell you all about it," I said.

～◦～

Mrs. Brisbane went back to the gym, and while we were alone, I described everything to Og. When I told him the part about Ms. Lark, he hopped up and down, saying, "BOING-BOING-BOING-BOING!"

And when I told him about Joey's dad and the cheering at the end, he dived into the water and splashed happily.

Then, I rested while I waited.

My friends all went home with their families, but Mr. and Mrs. Brisbane came back to Room 26 to pick up Og and me.

Mr. Brisbane was chuckling as they entered the room. "You certainly put on a show that no one will forget," he said. "Not as long as they live."

"You know who to thank for that," she said. "Humphrey. It seems that Daniel put him in his pocket for good luck."

"It turned out to be good luck after all," her husband agreed.

Mrs. Wright popped her head in the doorway. "Is the hamster all right?"

Mrs. Brisbane assured her that I was fine.

"Good thing I had *this*." Mrs. Wright fingered her whistle. "Have a wonderful holiday!"

And she popped her head out of the doorway again.

I have to say, I could have done without that whistle, but it was nice to hear that Mrs. Wright cared if I was all right.

The door opened again and Ms. Lark entered. "Sue, I'm so embarrassed about what happened," she said. "I apologize. I told the students to keep calm and focus. But I didn't follow my own advice."

"It turned out all right in the end," Mrs. Brisbane said. "But tell me, why are you so afraid of a little hamster?"

"I don't know," Ms. Lark said. "I've always been terrified of animals. My mother said I must have been scared by something furry when I was a baby."

"That's a shame," Mr. Brisbane said.

"I know," Ms. Lark agreed. "I wish I could change."

"Well, you can go on break now knowing you put on a great show," Mrs. Brisbane said.

"The children did all the work," Ms. Lark said.

"Oh, there you are!" Mr. Morales said from the doorway. He was wearing a candy-striped tie with his suit, and a Santa hat on his head.

"Congratulations," he told Ms. Lark. "You were right about the show. We'll have to do this every year."

"What about the part with the . . . hamster?" she asked.

Mr. Morales laughed so hard, his Santa hat shook. "Believe me, Mary, that was the best part of all!"

HUMPHREY'S WINTER WONDERINGS: I wonder how the show would have gone if Daniel hadn't put me in his pocket? It would have been entertaining . . . but not nearly as exciting!

Decking the Halls

Og and I have stayed at the Brisbanes' house many times.

But this time, it had changed completely. For one thing, there were tiny twinkling lights around the doors and windows. There was a wreath on the door and lights that looked like candles on the windowsills.

Inside, a gigantic tree took up a whole corner of the living room. It was covered with lights and little ornaments. I couldn't see them all from my cage on the table, but I did see elves and reindeer and shiny round things. And there were long strings of things draped all around the tree.

One was a string of cranberries.

The other was a string of popcorn.

Yum! I love popcorn!

There were long stockings hanging from the fireplace mantel. So that's the kind of stocking Holly was talking about!

There were decorations everywhere.

"Merry Christmas, Humphrey and Og," Mrs. Brisbane said as we got settled in. "Tomorrow will be a big day!"

She certainly wasn't exaggerating. The next morning, Mrs. Brisbane's sister arrived with her husband. There was a lot of hugging and talking and more hugging.

Then the doorbell rang and Mrs. Brisbane's niece and her husband arrived.

And with them were two children, a little younger than the students in Room 26. Once their coats were off and the suitcases carried inside, Mrs. Brisbane brought them over to meet us.

"Jenny and Todd, this is Humphrey. He's our classroom hamster!" she said.

"Pleased to meet you!" I squeaked.

Jenny and Todd giggled.

"And this is our classroom frog, Og," she continued.

"BOING-BOING!" Og said.

Jenny and Todd laughed out loud.

It was fun meeting new children. Jenny and Todd helped their Aunt Sue (that's what they called our teacher) and Uncle Bert (that's what they called our teacher's husband) take care of us. They even helped clean out my poo—and they didn't say "Ewww" once!

When Mrs. Brisbane took me out of the cage and put me in my hamster ball, Jenny and Todd loved following me all around the living room.

They also loved throwing Froggy Food Sticks into Og's tank.

Late that night, when it was time for bed, Mrs. Brisbane brought Jenny and Todd into the living room. They were both in their pajamas, ready for bed.

"Tonight, Santa will come with presents," she said. "And he'll fill these stockings for you."

"How will he know we're here and not home?" Jenny asked.

"Because Santa knows everything," Mrs. Brisbane said. "Don't worry, he'll be here. So we'd better leave out some cookies for him, and a glass of milk."

"And some carrots for Santa's reindeer?" Todd asked.

"Of course!" Mrs. Brisbane said. "They're working hard tonight."

"Did you hear that, Og?" I squeaked to my friend. "Yummy carrots?"

Og didn't answer, but I don't think frogs are very interested in carrots.

They put the food out right on the table next to us and headed for bed.

Right before she left the room, Mrs. Brisbane came over to my cage. "Remember the poem, Humphrey."

"What poem?" I squeaked.

"''Twas the night before Christmas, when all through the house, not a creature was stirring, not even a' . . . hamster!" Then she laughed and turned out the lights.

"That's a funny poem," I said to Og when we were alone. "*Hamster* doesn't even rhyme with *house*."

Og didn't seem to care about what rhymed and what didn't.

So I sat and I sat, looking at the stockings, looking at the tree, looking at the popcorn.

After a while, that popcorn looked more and more interesting to me. I like crunchy things. And I'd eaten popcorn once and liked it.

"Og, I don't think it would hurt if I went over and looked at the tree, do you?" I asked my neighbor.

Og splashed around a little. I wasn't sure whether that meant "yes" or "no."

A little while later, I said, "I won't touch anything. I'll just look at the ornaments."

Og splashed a little more, but it was hard to figure out what he meant.

So I finally made a decision. I jiggled the lock-that-doesn't-lock, threw open the door and scampered out of my cage.

"I'll be right back," I said.

The table we were on was low, so I easily slid down the leg and hurried over to the tree.

At first, I stood there and stared up at it. I'd never seen anything so glowing and glittery in my life!

Then I moved closer to look at the shiny, sparkly things.

The ornaments were fantastic! There was a tiny snowman. A jolly Santa. Lots of red and green and gold balls. There were apple ornaments and little houses.

And then there was the popcorn. Crispy, crunchy popcorn.

I scurried closer to the tree.

One of the popcorn strings almost touched the ground.

I thought it looked delicious. I thought it wouldn't hurt if I nibbled one tiny popcorn kernel. Then I didn't think any more.

I raced to the tree, stood on my tippy-toes and took a bite.

Oh, my! It was delicious! So I took another bite.

"BOING-BOING!" Og said. He has a way of warning me.

But I didn't see any danger. The room was empty and there was so much popcorn, the Brisbanes wouldn't miss a kernel or two.

CRUNCH-CRUNCH-CRUNCH!

It was as yummy as I imagined!

MUNCH-MUNCH-MUNCH!

And there was so much of it!

"BOING-BOING-BOING!" Og twanged.

"Just a few more bites," I squeaked back. I munched and crunched some more.

Then I heard a THUMP.

And I heard a BUMP!

I stopped munching and crunching and looked out at the room. There was a flash of red and a dash of white.

Somebody was there!

I froze mid-crunch. Who could it be?

The red moved. The white moved. I reached up to the branch above me and pulled my feet up.

If someone was nearby, that someone might think I was an ornament.

Thank goodness, Og was as quiet as a mouse.

The red-and-white figure stood in front of the fireplace and reached up to the stockings. Then the red-and-white thing moved to the table where my cage and Og's tank sat.

Paper rattled. Something thumped and bumped. Something clinked. Something crunched.

I heard some footsteps, and then I didn't see any red and white anymore.

I stayed frozen in place for a LONG-LONG-LONG time.

Even after I was sure the red-and-white figure had left, I waited and waited some more.

I have to admit, I did move when suddenly Og said, "BOING-BOING-BOING!"

What was Og trying to say?

"BOING-BOING!" he repeated.

I thought about it. Og was so quiet while the red-and-white thing was nearby. Maybe he was trying to tell me that we were alone again.

"Og, is the coast clear?" I squeaked.

"BOING!" he replied.

Og had never let me down before, so I took a chance.

I dropped from the branch and scampered across the floor toward the table.

"BOING-BOING!" Og twanged in an encouraging way.

When I got to the table, I needed a way to get back up. I was surprised to see a big pile of packages nearby that wasn't there before. I climbed them like steps up to the table and headed toward my cage.

As I hurried along, I passed by the plate of cookies, the glass of milk and the plate of carrots. And I noticed a strange thing.

The cookies were gone. The glass of milk was empty. And there were no carrots!

I knew Og hadn't taken them, but who had?

I was happy to be back in the safety of my cage again. I closed the door behind me.

"What happened, Og?" I squeaked. "Did you see who it was?"

"BOING-BOING-BOING-BOING-BOING!" Og replied. He was hopping and jumping and leaping around.

"Do you mean . . ." I paused to think. "Do you mean it was *Santa Claus*? Here?"

Og hopped and leaped and BOING-ed some more.

"It *could* have been," I said. "It *might* have been. It *must* have been Santa!"

I have to say, I was disappointed that I hadn't gotten a better look at him.

But I was also happy that he hadn't seen me.

"Santa came!" Todd and Jenny shouted the next morning. It was FUN-FUN-FUN to watch the family open presents and empty the stockings and laugh a lot.

While Jenny and Todd played with their presents, Mrs. Brisbane came over to our table and leaned in.

"You didn't think Santa would forget you, did you?" she asked.

Then she opened my cage and slipped in a wooden object. It looked like one of those dumbbells humans use to make themselves stronger.

"Merry Christmas, Humphrey," she said. "Here's something to chew on."

Jenny and Todd ran over to watch me sniff the new object.

I carefully bit into it. It was firm to the bite and a very fine thing to chew on!

"THANKS-THANKS-THANKS," I said.

Then she gently placed a very fine plant in Og's tank and said, "Merry Christmas, Og. This will make your house a little nicer and give you some shade."

Og dived into his water and said, "BOING-BOING-BOING!"

Jenny and Todd laughed every single time Og said something.

Then Mrs. Brisbane announced that she had *another* surprise for Og and me coming soon.

Later in the day, the doorbell rang, and when Mr. Brisbane opened the door—guess who was there?

It was Ms. Lark! And she was carrying her little keyboard with her.

"Thank you for inviting me," she said.

"Glad to have you, Mary," he said.

Before long, Mrs. Brisbane's whole family and Ms. Lark were sitting at the big dining room table. I could see them from the living room.

They ate a delicious-smelling dinner and they talked and laughed a lot.

After dinner, they gathered in the living room. Ms. Lark played some songs called "carols" on her keyboard and everybody sang. I especially enjoyed Ms. Lark's lovely voice.

Oh, they were wonderful songs. I especially liked one about decking the halls with boughs of holly.

"Fa-la-la-la-la, la-la-la-la!" everyone sang.

I joined in. "Fa-la-la-la-la, la-la-la-la!"

I even heard a "BOING-BOING!"

The humans stopped singing, but Og and I were still fa-la-la-ing.

Mrs. Brisbane heard us and laughed. "Mary, I think our friends Humphrey and Og like your songs," she said.

Ms. Lark shivered. "They're here?" she said. "You know I'm afraid of animals."

"Things can change," Mrs. Brisbane said. She motioned

to a spot on the couch next to the table we were on. "Why don't you come over here and watch them?"

"They're quite entertaining," Mr. Brisbane said. "Right, Humphrey?"

"Right!" I squeaked. If the Brisbanes wanted entertainment, I was the hamster to provide it.

First I climbed up to the tippy-top of my cage. "Watch carefully." Then I grabbed on to my tree branch and leaped from limb to limb.

"Oh, my!" Ms. Lark said.

Og hopped up and down under his plant. "BOING-BOING-BOING!"

Jenny and Todd laughed and I think I heard Ms. Lark laugh, too.

Not to be outdone, I scurried to my ladder bridge and walked across it to the other side of the cage. I climbed UP-UP-UP. This time, I hung from the top of the cage and made my way to the other side paw over paw.

"Look!" Ms. Lark said. "That's amazing!"

SPLASH! Og made a spectacular dive into the water side of his tank and began to swim.

"Oooh!" Ms. Lark exclaimed.

"Now, you don't think those lovable little animals would hurt you, do you?" Mrs. Brisbane said.

"May I hold Humphrey?" Jenny asked.

"Yes, but you have to be gentle," Mrs. Brisbane explained. "He's never bitten anyone so far, but if you move too fast and frighten him, he might."

Believe me, I wasn't about to bite Jenny!

Mrs. Brisbane showed her how to hold me cupped in one hand and told her to hold her other hand a few inches above my head, like a little roof.

I felt warm and cozy.

"Can I pet him, Aunt Sue?" Todd asked.

"Yes, if you stroke his back lightly with your finger," Mrs. Brisbane told him.

Oooh, that felt so good.

"He's soft," Todd whispered.

"How about you, Mary?" Mrs. Brisbane asked.

"Sure, go ahead!" I squeaked. I wiggled my whiskers to look extra-friendly.

She reached out slowly and rubbed her finger along my back. "Oh, yes, he is soft," she said. "And he's got such a cute face."

YES-YES-YES! I had won her over!

Two days ago, she'd been screaming at the sight of me. Now she was my friend.

A new friend really *is* the best gift of all.

After dinner, as everyone ate pie and chatted, Mrs. Brisbane said, "This has been the most perfect Christmas, celebrating with family and good friends. That includes you, Humphrey and Og."

"Gee whiz, come look out the window!" Mr. Brisbane called out. He'd been peeking through the curtains, but now he opened them wide.

Outside, snow was falling, covering the lawn, the sidewalk and the trees. The Christmas lights twinkled merrily against the falling snow.

"Oh, it's beautiful," Ms. Lark said.

"A white Christmas!" Jenny shouted. "We can build a snowman. And make snowflake ice cream!"

"Can you see it, Og?" I asked my neighbor.

"BOING-BOING!" Og replied.

"You know what it is? It's a winter wonderland," I told him.

I watched the snow and thought of what my friends were doing. Simon spinning his dreidel, Holly helping her grandparents, Sophie setting up the Nativity scene.

Harry was running all over the house with his cousins, while Paul F. ran his train around the tree.

Phoebe was talking on the phone to her parents—I was sure! And I imagined Kelsey was dreaming about dancing in *The Nutcracker*.

Thomas was singing carols, while Rosie and her family were eating yummy tamales.

Then there was Joey. He was with his dad. And he was happy.

I was happy, too. Happy to be a classroom pet and to be friends with so many GREAT-GREAT-GREAT humans and one funny frog. That's something I can celebrate every day of the year.

"FA-LA-LA-LA-LA!" I squeaked loudly. "LA-LA-LA-LA!"

HUMPHREY'S WINTER WONDERINGS: I wonder if I could EVER-EVER-EVER have a better holiday in my life!

Humphrey's Tips for Giving Gifts

1. Give someone a gift that they would like, not just something you like. For instance, I would not like a present that smells like stinky fish at all, but Og certainly would!

2. A handmade gift is always the best . . . unless you lose too much sleep over it.

3. The best gifts are the kind that can't be wrapped . . . like helping a friend.

4. Don't tell someone what to give you. Let them surprise you. Surprises are always fun!

5. The best time to give friends gifts is when they don't expect one.

6. It is far better to give that to receive. Giving Og a present gave me a HAPPY-HAPPY-HAPPY feeling!

7. Good things come in small packages . . . like hamsters, for instance.

8. A friend is a gift you give yourself. So I have lots of unsqueakably wonderful gifts!

9. A hug is a great gift. One size fits all and it can't be exchanged. (Although we hamsters prefer a soft stroke on the fur.)

10. If someone gives you a gift, please don't forget to squeak "Thank you!"